CARLOTTA MCBRIDE

Also by Charles Gorham

The Gilded Hearse
The Future Mr. Dolan
Trial by Darkness
Martha Crane
The Gold of Their Bodies
Wine of Life
McCaffery
Carlotta McBride
The Lion of Judah

CARLOTTA MCBRIDE

CHARLES GORHAM

CUTTING EDGE

ISBN-13: 978-1-962896-23-8

Published by
Cutting Edge Books
PO Box 8212
Calabasas, CA 91372
www.cuttingedgebooks.com

CONTENTS

CHAPTER ONE
EVENING IN APRIL

THE ROOM was painted an anonymous color, not quite grey, not quite beige, chosen, Carlotta had thought, because the doctor or the doctor's wife presumed this color to be undemanding of the tormented soul who found himself here in this room, day after day of his life, stealing back like a thief into the dreadful country of his past. The rug was beige and immaculate, with an underlining of foam rubber. The furniture—the doctor's desk, the three chairs, the neatly loaded bookcases—was of honey-colored wood. On the desk were a clean blotter, a clean pad of legal paper, a desk set made of fake onyx, fitted with an electric clock. At the edge of the desk, near the patient's chair, was an ash tray of the same onyx, always emptied and polished clean of any trace of the last patient, the warmth of whose body remained, however, in the beige cushion of the chair. Behind the desk were tall windows, hung with felt-lined beige curtains that nearly muted the sounds of traffic rising from the street below, where buses ran and taxis battled. Nothing was there to disturb, neither the colors nor the shapes nor the voice of the city heard through felt, faraway and unreal. The modern womb, Carlotta thought, the plastic womb, the womb with a view.

Behind the desk sat Doctor Fowler, himself anonymous as the color of his rug, neat, intelligent, almost serene, neuter as unsalted egg. On the wall behind Carlotta were documents lettered on parchment, testifying that Doctor Fowler once had existed outside this room, walked in the fragrance of Amherst, Massachusetts, burnt the medical student's oil on the banks of the Charles River. Sometimes, for Carlotta, it was impossible to believe it. He had always been here, Doctor Fowler, in this room, at that desk, with the silenced metropolis behind him, the noiseless clock in front of him sweeping away the expensive hour, minute by silent minute. He had neither past nor future but had himself been stopped in time, like a figure in a wax museum.

"How do you feel?" he asked now, leaning forward in his chair to reach for the long black fountain pen.

"I feel as if I were walking on a tight wire," Carlotta said, "wondering when I will fall off and whether or not I will hit the net."

He permitted himself to frown. "If you are really worried I think you should go on Antabuse," he said. "An incident at this time would not be helpful, you understand."

"Antabuse?" she said.

"Medication," he explained, taking a bottle from the drawer of his desk, handing Carlotta a fat white pill, on one side scored in the center, on the other marked with an A. She touched it with the tip of her tongue.

"It tastes like chalk," she said.

"It is harmless as chalk," the doctor said. "It is completely inert, you see, until it is in the presence of alcohol, in the human system."

"And then?"

"And then it is not harmless at all," said Doctor Fowler. "One vomits. His heart pounds. His face turns red. He falls to the floor. Sometimes, even, he dies." He shook a pill from the bottle, held it in the palm of his hand, and seemed to consult with it. "In this country," he went on, "there have been, I think, seven deaths associated with Antabuse. Of course, you must understand, most of these were suicides."

Carlotta tasted the pill again, then put it on the edge of the desk.

"Do you mean that if I swallow that pill, I cannot take a drink?" she said. "Unless I am willing to die for the drink?"

"Substantially, that's right," he said. "Though the chances of dying may be discounted."

"But this is a prison!" she exclaimed.

"Perhaps," the doctor said. "But it is a benign prison. And you always have the keys. Simply wait for five days and the prison ceases to exist." He offered her the bottle of pills and reached again for his pen. "If you would like to start tonight, I will write out the regime. It is simple."

Carlotta looked at the pill on the desk, staring at the blunt, cryptic A, thinking suddenly of Hester Prynne and the scarlet letter that Hester had embroidered with such defiant care. But I am no Mistress Prynne, she said to herself. No pain-worshiping Puritan I. The doctor's pen moved across the paper, the gilt point soundless against the crisp paper. Carlotta could taste rebellion in her mouth, the salt flavor of anger and fear, warm in her mouth like blood. In the bag on her lap was the letter. She had intended to talk about it. Now, with a surge of childish rebellion, she decided to say nothing about it. Bully me and see what it gets you, she said in her mind to Doctor Fowler. She pushed the bottle of pills toward him.

"No, thank you," she said. "I don't think I am quite ready to give up my free will."

Doctor Fowler fooled her. He cast off his neutrality, in the way a snake sloughs off its skin. "I think you are making a mistake," he said. "I advise you to think about it. At least take the pills with you and the directions."

"As you like," Carlotta said. She opened her purse. The letter from the firm of private detectives was there. She read the slogan under the name of the firm: INVESTIGATIONS DISCREETLY UNDERTAKEN. Then she put the pills and the prescription blank into her purse, closed the clasp firmly, and raised her head, looking at Doctor Fowler.

The buzzer attached to his desk purred to warn him that Carlotta's fifty minutes were almost used up and that the next patient waited in the ante-room, alone wih the Van Gogh prints, the bit of driftwood on the wall, the silent, indifferent tropical fish, the shop-worn copies of *Time* and *Life*. He stood up, neutral again, smiling his achromatic smile. "Well then, good night," he said.

Carlotta rose, all at once filled with fierce irrational resentment of the doctor and of his suave, monochromatic office. He is a fool, for all his degrees and his thirty dollars an hour, she said harshly to herself. Why am I here? How can he hold me, this castrato, unmanned by his own techniques, drained of color, tasteless, odorless, feeling nothing?

Aloud she said, "Well then, good night, Doctor."

He walked beside her to the office door. In the windowless waiting room a young man sat, staring incredulously at the tank of tropical fish. Doctor Fowler closed the door, eager, Carlotta supposed, to enjoy the ten minutes' respite that came between patients, ten minutes of solitude imposed with the senseless rigidity of a TV commercial.

She and the young man were alone in the little room that had six doors and no window. The bright, lacquered pictures on the wall were like brilliant, unfamiliar flags, genius and madness embedded in the color. The drone of the little engine that filtered the water for the tropical fish seemed to rise in pitch, like the motor of a dentist's drill. Resentfully, the young man looked up at Carlotta. He was soft-faced but dangerous, with an effeminate mouth and glossy black hair worn long at the sides and back, combed with relentless precision. He wore tight black trousers made of cotton gabardine, a sports shirt, a windbreaker. His shoes were new and square at the toes, fitted with metal cleats that gleamed in the doctor's inoffensive light. For kicking people to death in alleys, Carlotta thought, irrelevantly. This young man, this patient of Fowler's, was not one of those like herself who paid thirty dollars an hour in return for a captive audience of one. He must be one of the people from the clinic, part of Doctor Fowler's medical conscience. She stared at the boy quite rudely, wondering what had brought him into this claustrophile's room, into the presence of the noiseless fish and the steady, maddening drone of the motor. He stared back boldly then sneered, a self-confident, homosexual sneer, looking at the trim, expensive shoes, the trim, expensive dress, at the face that had enchanted and baffled skillful cameramen here and in Hollywood. It was a face sometimes poetic, sometimes almost sternly intelligent, sometimes fiercely passionate, always of extraordinary beauty, a face distinctly American, yet classic too and proud. Carlotta McBride was an actress and a good one; critics even had called her great, though she would not have agreed with them.

"I owe you any money, lady?" the boy in the windbreaker said in a perverted and hideous voice, a girl's voice somehow diseased. Carlotta noticed then the polish on his fingernails and the thin coating of rouge on his lips. She felt no pity. No compassion. Only blunt sexual contempt.

"Most improbable," she said, turning her face to the mirrored door, adjusting her hat.

"Bitch!" The boy spat out the word as if it were bitter on his tongue. "Bitch, bitch, bitch!"

The office door opened and Doctor Fowler's head appeared. His retreat had ended. The boy stood up, smoothed his hair, looked at Carlotta with hatred, then went into the doctor's office.

The door closed quietly, the latch making an efficient sound, the sound of a weapon being cocked. In the little room Carlotta stood, facing the reproduction of a Van Gogh painting called The Starry Night. St. Remy, her mind said. The tile-paved corridors of madness and the good, the compassionate Doctor Gachet, who loved pictures and the people who painted them, but whose love was all to nothing when it came to keeping Vincent out of the fatal cornfield, sky above heavy with the crows of death. To save Vincent they would have wanted another kind of scarecrow, Carlotta's mind said harshly.

Doctor Fowler had disturbed her with his intimations of close dangers, his offerings of prison pills. In the picture the pinwheel moon seemed to turn and to be coming toward her. She felt a weakness in the knees. Her mouth went dry. "I am sick, sick," she said in a whisper.

Her thighs tightened, the muscles firm as wood. She trembled, wanting to cry or to die or to be somehow swallowed up. Then, though she tried to fight it back, the hot urine spurted from her bladder, scalding her naked thighs, soaking the tops of her taut stockings. She forced her thighs to come apart and stood spread-legged on the fawn colored rug, no longer holding back, making a puddle that was soaked up by the nap of the rug, turning into a wet stain in the shape of a Rorschach blot.

"That is not the way to cry," she said aloud to the cruising fish. "Those are not tears, do you hear? but piss."

With her handkerchief she swabbed the insides of her thighs. Her stockings were wet and now the wet was turning cold. The puddle on the rug accused her. She looked at the dark tank of fish, on the side of which hung a little net. She took the net and managed to capture a brightly colored fish. One of the expensive ones, she thought, with a certain spasm of pleasure. She turned the net upside down and dropped the fish into the centre of the puddle she had made on the rug. She laughed, then giggled like a child on the edge of hysteria. I am clever, she thought. Certainly he will believe that the fish leaped out of the tank somehow, to make the wet place on his rug. What a brilliant idea!

She put the net back where she'd found it, then looked into the mirror again, offering to her reflection a long, slow, mysterious smile, a seductive smile, a thing she had learnt. Then, as she faced the mirror, there came from somewhere far away in

Doctor Fowler's apartment, through many rooms, the sound of a piano upon which a child was practicing scales. She stood still, her stockings wet, moving her fingers as the child moved hers. On the floor, the fish was dead. Carlotta's fingers moved alertly, up the keyboard, then down, down the keys, then up. The child faltered badly. Carlotta's fingers clenched into fists. "No, no, no!" she protested, under her breath. She hurried across the beige rug, out of the waiting room, fleeing in panic.

The self-service elevator moved slowly up the shaft, passing the floor, the red signal light winking. The airless hall was like a cell. Carlotta could not bear to wait for the elevator to make its descent. She opened the door behind her and hurried down the fire stairs, her heels making a hollow sound on the corrugated steel treads. In the fake Moorish lobby an astonished doorman stared at her, rising from his bench ... *"Hey, lady!"* She darted past him, through glass doors that led to the street, sensing that she had made an escape, from what she was not quite certain.

It was dusk. The street was crowded with people hurrying home from the subway kiosks and from the bus stop on the corner. She was on the West Side of New York in the Eighties, a part of town she visited only when she came to see Doctor Fowler. She was used to the East Side; the people here were unfamiliar, almost foreign to her. She might have been in another city or perhaps in Brooklyn. It was early spring, a warm night. Men carried topcoats on their arms. A Puerto-Rican girl passed by, wearing a bright tropical print. The street dipped toward the shore line and there was a glimpse of sun on the river.

Carlotta walked to the corner where the broad cross street joined an avenue choked with buses, taxis and cars, all moving toward the north. Halfway up the block burned a neon sign, the round-cornered letters a heatless red: MURPHY'S—BAR & GRILL. Carlotta shuddered, standing on the corner. Over her head, with a clicking sound, the traffic light changed color. A taxi braked with a scream, then backed out of the crosswalk. The subway crowd crossed the street. Carlotta stood in the path of the crowd, bumped and pushed by hurrying people. Then she turned suddenly and walked toward the neon sign, her purse held close to her body, as if it contained some secret of importance. She detested Doctor Fowler for having mentioned that damned pill, that prison pill. She checked herself in the street, forcing her mind into focus. When had she really decided to go into a bar? she wondered. At the moment she read the letter, this morning, when Katie brought the mail on the tray that held her breakfast? An hour later? An hour ago? Certainly not in the few minutes while she sat with Doctor Fowler's pill in her hand, thinking of Hester Prynne. Oh, no. Nor had it been in the waiting room, when she had soiled the floor and then murdered the doctor's fish. She was terrified and she was helpless. She turned with a swift, military movement and walked through the open door of the bar.

It was an ordinary neighborhood bar, with a new floor made of plastic tile and stools covered with red leatherette, artificial, enormous mushrooms fashioned out of plastic and chrome. Behind the bar, against the mirror, gleamed the brightly labeled bottles, Scotch and bourbon to the right, blended whiskey and gin to the left, in the center two bottles, unopened, of French brandy. The bartender was an old man, red-faced, wearing a clean white shirt and apron.

"Yes, miss?"

Carlotta thought for a moment, then asked for vodka. It was supposed to leave no smell, she remembered from the advertising; perhaps if she had only one or two, no one would know the difference. The bartender poured from a bottle that had a Polish eagle on the label. "On the side, miss?" he said.

"Water," said Carlotta. Her heart was pounding.

The bartender put ice into a glass, washed the ice, then covered it with water. Quietly, he said, "We got booths in the back, miss. Maybe you'd be more comfortable like, sitting down, instead of here."

"I am not going to stay long enough to make it worth while sitting down," said Carlotta firmly.

She put a dollar on the bar and the change was placed beside her glass. For some minutes, ten, perhaps, or fifteen, she stared at the little glass of vodka, clear and innocent as water, only the faintest oiliness betraying the fact that half of it was grain neutral spirits, alcohol to you, she thought. Six months, her mind whispered, entering into a kind of debate with her conscience. Six months of sitting in Doctor Fowler's beige room, first on the couch, then in the patient's chair, with its sponge rubber pad on the seat, its shiny arms that were sometimes moist with the sweat of the last person's palms. Six months of going to parties, watching the other people drink, sipping warm ginger ale from a highball glass, trying to be nice, nice, nice, while all the others got pleasantly mulled in their non-pathological fashion. Six months of quietly turning the wine glass upside down in all the best French restaurants, of making excuses for being sober, of staying home, trying to read, going alone to movies, movies, movies, until her eyes were blurred, her mind sogged with the foolish stories. Movies! she thought. My God, how I loathe movies!

She drank the vodka in one gulp. It burnt more than she had expected and there was a rancid taste. Her stomach turned in protest. Her eyes flooded. She swallowed a mouthful of ice water and dabbed at her eyes with her handkerchief, then remembered that she had used it to wipe the urine from her thighs. She touched her nose with the handkerchief and sniffed. The smell of urine was very strong. She put the handkerchief into her bag and asked politely for another drink. The warmth spread through her body. Her lips were slightly and pleasantly numb. She had passed through the moral customs barrier and entered a dangerous country. She was aware of anticipation, a bright reckless sense that there was adventure waiting for her beyond the next turning. To her it was a familiar sensation, a headiness and conviction of gallantry somewhat similar to what one feels at the controls of a powerful motor car, beginning a long night journey at high speed under the stars, splitting the dark and liquid night with the high beams, conscious of thrilling power. She drank the second vodka, sat on one of the mushroom stools, and ordered a third.

Men came into the bar, workingmen from the neighborhood, drinking beer, mostly, or whiskey with beer for a chaser. Boilermaker, she said to herself, her fingers engaged with the vodka glass in a kind of possessive caress. The men ignored her, but she was aware of hostility. This was a neighborhood bar, a place that did not care for strangers, especially when the stranger was a woman. When women came into this bar it was not to drink, but for the purpose of reclaiming husbands from the threatening masculine world.

When she had finished the third vodka, Carlotta took it for granted that she would go on drinking. She could not stop now, unless she were locked in a cell or tied to the bed in a hospital room. She felt a wave of fear and shuddered in the way one shudders after a strong straight drink. She glanced at her watch, then selected two dimes from the arrangement of change on the bar, got down from the stool and made her way deliberately to the telephone booth in the rear of the saloon. There was a kitchen behind a pair of swinging doors. The odors of cabbage and frying meat struck her suddenly and made her gag. What idiot, she asked herself, wrote the law that obliges a barroom to serve hot meals?

She dialed Wally Martin's number, after looking it up in her little book. While the phone rang at the other end she took a deep breath and steadied herself against the phone booth shelf. When Wally answered she stood up straight in the booth and altered her voice, sounding as if she suffered from laryngitis or a heavy cold.

"Wally, darling, I meant to call you earlier," she apologized in a pathetic croak. "But they've given me some kind of mycen thing and the stuff put me to sleep."

"Will you be able to go on?" asked Wally sympathetically. He was young for a stage manager and one of Carlotta's admirers.

"Oh darling not tonight," she said helplessly. "But I should be fine by tomorrow. It's a twenty-four hour thing, I should think, and these drugs are marvelous."

"First performance you've missed," said Wally indulgently. "Go back to sleep, Miss McBride. I'll call Sabra right away."

That was her understudy, Sabra Sherman. Carlotta felt a flash of resentment and of something related to guilt. Into the phone she said, "Tell her the best of luck from me, the sweet little thing."

"Take care of yourself," said Wally.

"I shan't move from bed," she promised.

She hung up and sat in the booth for a few minutes, her hand on the phone in its cradle. Then she dialed her apartment. The bell rang three times before Katie answered in her fine high brogue.

"Katie, listen to me," Carlotta said briskly. "If anyone calls—the theater, or Mr. Falkstein, or anyone else—I am sick in bed and asleep and I cannot be disturbed, do you understand?"

There was a long silence, then Katie said, "Miss McBride, don't do it." She was younger than Carlotta but she had been raised in a drunkard's house in the hills of Donegal. She feared "the creature" and understood it in elementary fashion.

"It's not what you think," Carlotta said. "It's just that I've got to have a night off and this is the only way I can get it, by pretending. I'm tired, Katie. Dog tired. Six months of that part are enough to put Charles Atlas on the floor."

"All right, Miss McBride, I'll be here when you get home," Katie said.

She doesn't believe me, thought Carlotta. She doesn't believe me at all. Probably Wally didn't believe me either. And there was Falkstein. She thought suddenly of Falkstein's face as it would be when Wally Martin told him she wasn't going on tonight. Falkstein was the producer. He made it a principle of business to believe nothing, nothing at all, not even Bible truth. She recalled to herself Falkstein's words, uttered six months ago when he was casting the play. "All right, angel, the part's yours. It's made for you. It was written for you," he had said. Then he had looked at his cigar. "But remember this, angel child. One slip and it's all over, even if I have to close the play when we're doing standing room business." There had been polish on his fingernails and polish on his thinning hair; he had meant every word he said.

Carlotta sighed and her head sank forward, touching the metal coinbox. At this moment, she knew, the line was forming at the box office, people waiting to pay for the privilege of standing for two and one half hours to see Carlotta McBride in what everyone agreed was the greatest, hottest hit in town, except, of course, for the musical shows. Thinking of Falkstein and of the people outside the theater, Carlotta had a wave of self-loathing, or was it simply self-pity? She bit her lower lip, aware of a forming cloud of depression that almost touched her. She straightened up in the telephone booth. "I need another drink," she said, deliberately and aloud, her voice hollow in the closed-up booth. She got up, shook out her skirt, and went back to the bar. A man stood where she had been sitting, one arm on the bar, staring moodily at his beer. "Excuse me," said Carlotta politely, touching his hand. Sullenly he moved away, carrying his glass of beer. Carlotta sat on the plump stool and ordered another drink. Before she drank it, she was bored. This place is intolerable, she thought. I must get out. She gulped the drink, left her change on the bar, and hurried through the barroom door into the pleasant April night.

At the curb she stopped, wondering where she wanted to go. She should not be seen tonight in any of the places where she would meet theatrical people or columnists. She had made up her mind that what she needed was one good night on the town and she didn't intend to give them a chance to start any rumors. Sardi's, Billingsley's, Twenty-one—places like that were out. So were the dozens of little bars, in the side streets in the Fifties and Sixties. What then was left?

Third Avenue, she replied.

But last time she had promised herself that never again would she set foot in a Third Avenue saloon. Standing at the curb in the calm spring evening, she had a vivid memory of that night back in the past when they had carried her out of Mickey Sheridan's saloon to an ambulance that stood in the street with its red lights flashing, remembering the cool masculine contempt on the face of the young policeman, the smooth, scarcely shaven face of a corrupted altar boy. She remembered the Bellevue sheets that smelled of something like lysol—and the hideous faces in the ward around her when she woke up in the morning, sick to her stomach, hardly able to walk as far as the toilets at the end of the ward.

"Third Avenue," she said out loud. It was a place where you finished, not the place where you began. But what was left, if you ruled out all the places on the Broadway columnists' circuit? What was left was Mickey Sheridan's, no longer in the shadow of the "El," it was true, but still Mickey Sheridan's, good old Mickey Sheridan's, a saloon for drunks, run by a drunk. Of, by, and for drunks, said Carlotta to herself.

"Taxi!" she called, in her clear, splendid voice. "Taxicab!"

The cab was a small one that smelled of newness and a cheap cigar. She gave the driver the address and took a cigarette from her case. Holding the lighter, her hand trembled. Strange, she thought. After three drinks I should be as steady as a rock. No, it had been four drinks, she corrected herself. It was too early to lose count. Much, much too early. She drew deep on the cigarette and held the smoke in her lungs. Relax, she counseled herself. Sit back in the cab and relax. After all, everyone is entitled to a night off. Besides, it isn't a bad idea to have little Sabra What's-her-name? walk through the part for once. After a while, when a show has settled down, they begin to take you for granted.

Not a bad idea at all to remind them of just who it is that keeps those seats filled with cash carrying asses, just who it is, after all, that keeps them standing in the back of the house, craning their necks and straining their ears, just so they can say that they've seen Carlotta McBride.

The cab stopped for a traffic light at Park Avenue. Long, costly automobiles passed in review. Well-dressed women were walking dogs. The city was benign in the evening light. Carlotta tossed away the stub of her cigarette, then covered her face with her hands. I am my own master, a voice inside her seemed to insist. I can get out of this cab and walk to my own apartment, have a warm bath and a warm milk and get into a warm bed, alone, except for a new book. I can walk through the city for hours if I like and go home when I please to a sleep of exhaustion. I can call AA Intergroup, find a meeting and go to it, give them a cheap little thrill when I stand up on the platform and say: "My name is Carlotta McBride and I'm an alcoholic." Even, if I like, I can get to the theater just before curtain time, tell them I've taken a turn for the better and break little Sabra Sherman's heart. I can do what I please, and no one is going to put me in prison by giving me fat white pills that I don't want to take, as if I had no will of my own, no mind of my own at all. I am Carlotta McBride and I am my own master.

The lights changed and the cab moved eastward toward Third Avenue, turning its back on the glass houses and bronze houses that stood like a series of model prisons along the glossy street.

Mickey Sheridan was behind the bar, a long-nosed Irishman, thin as a sparrow, always the spoilt priest, with daughters in the best of Catholic schools and a wife who had been the prettiest girl in her class at the College of Mount Saint Vincent.

"Good evening, Carlotta."

"Good evening, Mickey."

The greeting was cheerful, the pale blue eyes were friendly. It was as if there had never been that night of the ambulance and the young, self-righteous policeman. That is my Mickey, Carlotta thought, himself a member of the lodge. He understood certain things no outsider could understand ever in this world.

"I will have Irish whiskey, if you please." She uttered the words with a slight brogue. "On the rocks, if you'll be so kind."

"At your service, me lovely lady."

Mickey's brogue was fake as her own; he had been born in Hartford, Connecticut. Still, he had lived in Ireland, which was more than she had done.

She sipped the whiskey, enjoying the smell, thinking: this is more like it. Vodka may have no smell, but to me it is like medicine, not like liquor at all. She was a whiskey drinker. Her first drink had been Irish whiskey, with lots of ice and fizz water and not very much whiskey at all. It had been mixed by Michael McBride and she had sat on his lap to drink it.

She thought of him now and she trembled, just as she always trembled, her soul flooded with hot shame, the muscles of her thighs rigid. She opened her handbag and took out the letter from the detective agency. In the depths of her bag, with her lipstick and mirror, was the bottle of prison pills Doctor Fowler had given her. She closed the bag emphatically and unfolded the letter:—"Beg to inform you that subject has been located in Paris, France. We await further instructions."

Paris, France, she understood, was ten hours from Idlewild, according to the advertising. Why hadn't she asked Falkstein for two nights off and gone to Paris safe and sober? That was what she had intended to talk to Doctor Fowler about, when she said she was walking on a tight wire. But Doctor Fowler had been stupid enough to offer her those fat white pills. "Nazi therapy," she said out loud, putting the letter back in her bag.

She finished her drink and asked for another, taking the second one more slowly. Sheridan's was almost empty. At the end of the bar, Pat Keeley dozed over a glass of whiskey and milk an old sailor of the Royal Navy, dying of throat cancer, filled with alcohol and reluctance to die. "As life what is so sweet?" recited Carlotta to herself. "What creature would not choose thee?" In the booth they called Lower Three, slept the professional gentleman, Beauregard Johnson, wearing, as he always did, the rosette of the Society of the Cincinnati. In another booth sat Sheridan's chef, wearing a filthy apron, puzzling out the *Daily News*. Above these two, on the dirty wall, a colleen wore a perpetual smile, beckoning to all in view: *cead mile fáilte.* COME TO IRELAND IN THE SPRINGTIME. Behind the bar sat Sheridan himself, silently reading Tacitus in the original, from a book that was bound in good leather. It was not an affectation. He enjoyed reading Latin and his hand-bound classics had been picked up cheap from a dealer on Fourth Avenue.

He was a periodical drunkard.

When the thing came on him, always of a sudden, he would take off the apron of office, phone to the union for a substitute bartender, and sit himself down in Lower Three with two bottles of Irish whiskey, one for himself and one for the leeches who almost at once were swarming around him. When he had finished the bottle he would take the cash that was in the register—always a considerable sum—and call for a Carey Cadillac to drive him to Hartford, Connecticut, to the seminary that had thrown him out when he was twenty-two years old and an eager young Latinist on the nights when he wasn't drinking.

"Come out of there, Father Curran, and fight," he would bellow at the old stone fortress of a building, when the Carey car had got him there. "Come into the street, I defy you, Father, take off your collar and fight like a man with Joseph Michael Aloysius Sheridan, that you ruined his life these twenty years and turned into a helpless drunkard."

Old Father Curran had been dead for a decade. To Sheridan it made no difference. His war with the Catholic Church was a war with Father Curran, in Hartford or in Heaven. Sometimes they would call the police and Sheridan would sleep in a cell. Sometimes an old priest would lead him into the seminary and give him a narrow bed for the night. In the morning, bleary-eyed, Sheridan would go to Mass, leave a check for a hundred dollars and carry on with his drunk that would last until he collapsed on the floor of his wife's pretty bedroom and the doctor had been sent for to put him to sleep with a hypodermic needle, while his handsome, troubled daughters in their neat blue blazers pretended they did not understand the nature of his illness.

Now he sat reading his Latin, waiting for the evening's rush of business that should begin in half an hour. He was a monogamist, Sheridan, a good husband and father, a Catholic, and a fatalist who believed in the slogan printed on his books of paper matches: TAKE IT EASY.

From her station at the end of the bar, Carlotta looked at Sheridan and smiled at him with some affection. He was a publican, she was a patron, and between them stood the literal bar, but they were also friends in an odd, parenthetic sense; without ever having talked very much, it was understood between them that they hated and loved the same things. And there was also the bond of drink, allegiance of the afflicted or the blest, according to the calendar or the point of view.

Sheridan paused in his reading, took up a Latin dictionary, searched for a word and found it. He put the dictionary back on the shelf beside the aspirin and the ink bottle, closed his elegant Tacitus, stood up and stretched his starched white arms. "Latin me that, you Trinity scholard," he said in a reedy Joycean brogue. "Anna Livia, *alla aluvial.* That and the convent napkins twelve." He moved swiftly up the bar to fix a drink for Carlotta. "Do you never regret having been deprived of the graces that come with a classical education?" he asked cheerfully, swabbing clean the dirty bar before he put Carlotta's drink beside her hand.

"I do, Michael, that I do," answered Carlotta, in her expert, fraudulent brogue.

Sometimes she and Sheridan played at being Irish—music hall Irish or James Joyce Irish or Easter Week Irish, with staunch rebel hearts and pistols under their trench coats. She was the Countess Markiewitz, Sheridan was Cathal Brugha. Carlotta knew the drill. One summer at Stockbridge she had played Pegeen Mike and brought the echoes of the Dublin Abbey to the slicked-up New England town. Synge and his Western imagery had drawn her into infatuation with romantic Ireland, and that summer she had read all the Irish literature on the shelves of the village library—Synge and O'Casey, Yeats and O'Connor, Lady Gregory, early Joyce, O'Flaherty, and a thin, strange book by a man who called himself Miles Na gCopaleen.

Back in New York that autumn she had haunted the Irish shop on Madison Avenue that sold books and tea and Saints' pictures, blackthorn sticks and Donegal tweed, where two respectable Catholic spinsters—the proprietors—plotted bloody but sexless revolution and—Praise be to Almighty God—safe deliverance to the Faith of the six stolen counties.

In Carlotta's apartment was a file of Irish rebel songs on records, unplayed now for more than a year, and tucked away in a drawer were photographs of various martyrs: MacSwiney, Cathal Brugha, Padraic Pearse and the rest, all of them bought from the old maids, handed to her in a plain wrapper, as if this were Belfast itself and owning a photo of Terence MacSwiney would get you a year in a British cell.

It was a phase that had passed, this obsession with Ireland, but it remained as an underlayer, sometimes stirred by alcohol.

"Good men and true in this house who dwell
To a stranger boucle I pray you tell. ... "

Softly, Carlotta sang to herself, both hands on her glass.

"The Croppy Boy," said Sheridan brightly.

"Up the Rebels," said Carlotta.

Irish, she said to herself. Who was it that called them the cry-babies of the western world? Heywood Broun, she thought. Somebody like that, dead for a long time. I am Carlotta McBride, she said patiently to herself. Educated by the gentle nuns, dressed in the best blue serge was I, even if there were lace panties beneath the convent uniform, lovely, prohibited underwear, silk that was soft as sin itself, delightfully wicked to the touch of my scrubbed and unmanicured convent hand. Ah, the lovely fires of sin, smouldering always in the chaplain's sermons, young Father Mulligan, the half-back from Holy Cross; a young priest, they supposed, better to understand the young. I am Carlotta McBride. Irish? Perhaps. Catholic? Perhaps. What on this good earth am I? she asked herself now in Sheridan's Bar. Am I Irish? German, perhaps? Russian, maybe. I have the eyes. I might be Jewish or old Yankee, or filled with the blood of the gallant South.

She shook her head and rejected this. I somehow cannot cast myself as the sister of Scarlett O'Hara, even the sister under the skin. "The South is out," she said aloud, lifting her empty glass and asking for another drink.

The place was beginning to fill up. There was Panther, the huge Negro, once a preliminary prizefighter, now serving as second mate on one of those garbage trucks that aren't owned by the city. Private Sanitation, that was it. What a curiously intimate name.

At the end of the bar, ash-grey, sat the woman they called The Duchess, drinking rum and Coca-Cola, aware of her own sickly grandeur, proud as a French aristocrat waiting for the guillotine in the Prison of La Force, and terribly careful still of her hands. Near her were two cruising boys, dressed in the current sepulchral mode, charcoal grey, charcoal brown, charcoal green, charcoal white. Carlotta could see their slim, Italianate shoes, obscene as an article of feminine hygiene left by mistake on the bathroom shelf. Why do I dislike them so? Carlotta asked herself. I am no moralist, nor do I think that sex must be limited to à la papa. Certainly I should be armed with sympathy for those who have been wounded, *les blessés de la vie*, bruised in the womb or elsewhere. Yet dislike them she did and especially when she had been drinking.

They stared at her, both of them, and one whispered to the other, "I tell you, darling, it can't be. She's on stage at this moment." He looked at the black-faced watch on his wrist and nodded firmly. "Besides, the mouth is completely wrong." The other one shrugged disinterestedly and both of them turned away. Carlotta was unperturbed. She was used to being stared at in bars and restaurants and theater lobbies. Then suddenly she was struck by a pang of guilt. Why am I here? she asked herself, looking at her own watch. They are now in the middle of the second act, just at the place where I turn and admit to my husband that I have slept with the prize-fighter. They should have made him a bull-fighter, she said contemptuously to herself. Or better still, a bull. She hated this play, that everyone else said was a work of genius. She looked at the two homosexuals and frowned. The playwright was one of them, southern school, southern style. Scent of magnolia, sweet and fresh, then the sudden smell of rutting flesh. Rut, rut, rut. I, Carlotta, am never in rut, for man or boy or bull, man. Rut, hog or die. I am never in rut, but a rut I'm in.

She watched a melting ice cube turn indolently in her glass, then noiselessly, not moving her lips, she began in her mind to read the lines of the play, almost at the instant they were being read on stage by that little incompetent bitch Sabra Sherman, who would never, she said, never make an actress as long as she lived, poor thing. She read straight through to the final curtain, seeming to hear the applause at the end as she had been hearing it most nights during these last months.

She raised her head and looked around her, realizing that she was quite drunk. The bar was crowded—three deep—and there was a steady blur of voices, broken suddenly by a peal of semi-hysterical laughter. Carlotta pinched her forearm, reassured when she felt pain. At least I am not feeling no pain, she said.

The faces came into focus.

There was Arthur the Artist, clinging to a glass of flat beer, waiting for someone who would volunteer to buy him a real drink. Beside him was the man who taught the impoverished blind to walk without walking into things. Once she had seen him in the street, leading a blind boy by the arm, a Negro boy with a white cane and a stoical African face. Some days you must misjudge and go to your work when you are drunk, she had said to him once. Blind drunk leading the blind. God takes care of fools and drunkards. He does not take care of the blind.

For some minutes she watched Arthur and his sad unfinished beer. She was aware of the need to perform some act of kindness. Always when she drank she was the Lady Bountiful. She sought out people like Arthur the Artist. Why? she wondered. To get rid of the money in her purse would do her no good. There was always credit, and there was always more money at home. Still, she knew that she would succumb to the need to give something away. And Arthur the Artist sat waiting for someone who felt the need to be generous. It was his function in life, to be the recipient of kindness, the object of benevolence. He existed on this earth as a receptacle for kindness. It was his profession. He was a frockless mendicant, an unlicensed but symbolic beggar. Alms and the man I sing. Yet there was protocol. One did not simply hand him money as if he were a beggar in the street. First it was necessary to play the role of friend, equal, and intellectual confidante.

Carlotta got down from her stool and walked past the machine that sold nuts for a penny, moving carefully through the crowd. She nodded to people who greeted her, kissed someone on the cheek, refused a drink, and at last reached the place where stood Arthur with his tepid beer. She touched his shoulder. "Carlotta McBride!" They embraced. The sick eyes blinked at her from behind grotesque lenses. He smelt of turpentine. Odd, she thought. He can't be working. He has not worked for years. Perhaps he dabs a bit of turps behind his ears like perfume to help make the effect.

They found an empty booth in the back and sat down. On the wall beside them were the Lakes of Killarney in glorious ektachrome; a travel poster: *An Tostel:* Ireland of the Hundred Thousand Welcomes. *Cead mile fäilte.* Will you come to the bower?

"Well, Arthur, may I buy you a drink to celebrate my night of freedom?" said Carlotta cheerfully.

"I won't refuse," said Arthur, swallowing the mouthful of beer he had carried with him. She gave him a five dollar bill and he went to the bar for drinks. "I got doubles," he said when he returned, handing her the change. "Madison Avenue seems to have taken over Sheridan's tonight."

It was true. The place was crowded with young advertising men and press agents, who came here to drink because they understood that somehow this filthy bar was chic. There were two kinds of faces; the shiny, muffin-face, rude with the glow of a healthy childhood, and the semi-saturnine face, dark and carefully shaven. Both were sexless as toothpaste.

"Nowadays Love comes in Tubes," Carlotta said.

Arthur blinked at her. "At last," he said. "A fully disposable Love Object."

"Close cover before striking match," she said.

So they talked for an hour, talking under the jukebox blare, sometimes in gibberish, sometimes quite with good sense. When someone was being kind to him, Arthur drank with extraordinary speed—vodka with beer for a chaser. Carlotta drank along with him, trying not to look at his eyes, for the cataracts were coming back behind the lenses that were thick as saucers. To be a painter with cataracts! It was a god-given reason for drinking. Who could quarrel with tragedy when it was so simplistic, almost so simple-minded?

"You smell of your trade," Carlotta said. "Are you working then, Arthur?"

"Restoring a picture," he said. "I need the money badly."

It was her cue, she understood. She gave him a twenty dollar bill which he took without comment, folding it carefully before he stowed it in the waist pocket of his corduroy trousers.

"How is Gloria?" Carlotta asked politely.

Gloria was his wife, a patient, Jewish girl from the Bronx.

"Most unhappy," Arthur said. He took a document from his pocket and handed it to Carlotta. "That came in the mail this morning," he said morosely.

It was a notice of eviction, typed on a standard form that the landlord buys in a stationery store. Carlotta wrinkled her nose, scanning a few sentences of the awful language. She detested legal documents and had an irrelevant loathing for lawyers.

"I will keep it," she said, putting the paper into her purse beside Doctor Fowler's pills and the letter from the detective agency. Arthur shrugged helplessly. Carlotta sent him to the bar for drinks. After a little he went away, pretending to have some errand or other.

Where will he go? Carlotta wondered. Will he go home to his wife and child with the twenty dollars I gave him, take them out to a cafeteria and fill them both with food? Or will he simply go down the street to Moriarity's or the Yukon, to stand alone at the bar and drink, filled with splendid independence, solvent and disobliged to submit to anyone's conversation, freed, while the money lasts, of the obligation to listen that infected him like a curse? Carlotta shrugged. It doesn't matter, she said to herself. She had given him something. An act of kindness had been performed. With its product she had no concern.

Alone now, she sat in the booth, her back to the bar and its crowd, using the buzzer when she wanted a drink. After some time, she got up and went to the ladies' room. The spring hinges creaked as she opened the door. On the stool sat a middle-aged woman with strawberry-colored hair, asleep or dead, motionless. Carlotta shrugged and went next door to the men's room. The mustard colored walls were adorned with graffiti, some old, some new. There was an ammoniac reek mixed with the cloying perfume that rose from a block of pink disinfectant steeping in the bottom of the urinal. The closet with the toilet bowl was locked, because the fairies used it. It was necessary to get a key from the bar. Carlotta squatted in front of the urinal, pulling her skirts up high and spreading her legs. She felt the salt spray on her face. She stood up, smoothing her skirt, reading a notice that had been scraped with a knife into the dirty plaster: IF YOU LIKE BOY-HUMP I AM THE ONE FOR YOU. 59 ST. SUBWAY UPTOWN FOUR O'CLOCK.

She went out of the little room, frowning over what she had read. Does he go every day to the same subway toilet? she wondered. At the same hour? Does advertising really work? Are there customers on hand? Does anyone read what I have read and Act Now! as the ads demand? Is there a queue every day at four o'clock in the Fifty-ninth Street Subway toilet, just as there is a queue for me every day at the box office?

She sat in her booth, feeling intensely clinical, as if she watched a metropolis of ants. The crowd at the bar had thinned out. Two plainclothes policemen chatted with Sheridan, guns bulging under their coats. To Carlotta they nodded respectfully, tipping their hats. They are good standard policemen, she thought, the kind who are sent to the theater when someone misses a piece of jewelry, not like that supercilious policeman who sneered at me when they carried me out of here on a stretcher. She had a sense of self-confidence now. Under her breath, she began to sing:—

> Old Mountjoy, one Monday morning,
> High upon the gallows tree,
> Kevin Barry gave his young life,
> For the cawse of libertee.

She was singing to herself, softly, a genuine tear in her eye, performing a kind of emotional masturbation that was soothing and reassuring. She was lost in her own boozy world, alone with a secret self.

There was a hand on her arm. "Don't cry, beautiful. Life is for kicks, don't you know that?" He was a big man with a fleshy face, wearing an expensive tweed jacket; Harvard clubman type, running to fat.

"Please don't touch me!" said Carlotta sharply.

"Ah, don't be like that."

Then the hand was on her breast, the fat face close to hers.

"Stop it!" she cried out.

Like hunting dogs the two detectives turned at the sound of her voice. Almost at once they were down the bar and stood beside Carlotta's booth.

"Leave the lady alone, jack," one of them said quietly.

"Says who?" the big man asked, turning, ready to fight, as if a fight was what he really sought, rather than Carlotta's breast.

"Says we," said the detective.

The big man swung his fists. Like vicious snakes the black-jacks rose in the air and descended, once, twice, three times. The man staggered back, bleeding from both cheeks. One of the detectives showed his badge.

"Get out of here, mac, before you get hurt," he said without emotion. "Go on home where you belong."

The big man seemed to sag. He looked first at one policeman, then at the other, his eyes filled with hurt and shock. Then he turned and plodded to the door, a handkerchief held to his bleeding face.

Carlotta was sick to her stomach. "He touched me," she said to the policeman. "I don't mind that he spoke to me, you understand, but he touched me with his hand."

"He won't bother you any more, Miss McBride," one of the policemen said.

"Wise guy," said the other one.

They touched their hats. The blackjacks dangled from their wrists, phallic, bright with blood. They put them away and returned to the bar to finish their drinks. After a few minutes they said good night to Sheridan and left. In the bar was a dead silence. Carlotta gagged. It was the blood that made her ill. Blood always made her ill. Virgin's blood. She remembered the blood and the uniform blouse carelessly hung on a straight-backed chair, medal ribbons bright and romantic in the pale gold of the evening sun, winter sun in New England, sifting through the slats of the blinds, pretty military ribbons speaking of beautiful distant battles, Virgin's blood in the Yankee sun and the sweet pain of torn flesh, a wicked looseness in the thighs, the taste of champagne mixed with the taste of flesh and tobacco, the bite of day old whisker on the soft flesh of her breast, and then the guilt of mortal sin, the hot tears that would not fall, the trembling chill of mortal fear, the cry of anguish never uttered, the unspoken appeal for help.

"Daddy! Daddy!"

She was weeping quietly, elbows on the table. Sheridan brought her another drink. "Four o'clock, Carlotta," he said, politely ignoring her tears. "Time to sweep the old place out."

She finished the drink quickly, offered to pay, and was told it was on the house.

"Good night then Mick," she said, when she was at the door.

"Good night, Your Grace," called Sheridan.

She stepped into the street. At four in the morning the air was crisp. She took a deep breath. Behind her, Sheridan was locking the door. She was quite steady on her feet and wide awake now, in the fresh night air. The thought of going to bed was distasteful. She had been through the routine before. Two nembutals, pierced with a pin to make them work faster, warm milk with nutmeg on it, sometimes even a warm bath, and then the hideous, sleepless bed, a torture table made of foam rubber upon which one writhed in anguish, whimpered, sobbed, bit the pillow, or cried out hysterically to the indifferent dark.

To the north were the lights of a taxicab that cruised slowly down the street. She stepped out from the curb and hailed it, giving the driver an address that made him turn in his seat and protest: "Lady, I got a living to make."

"I will give you five dollars over what is on the meter when we get there," Carlotta said firmly. "You can ride back empty."

"Okay lady, it's your money," the driver said cheerfully, putting the car into gear and making a U-turn, heading north for the after-hours place on the fringe of Spanish Harlem. Carlotta knew a dozen such places, some of them in the east Fifties, some in the Village, but all of those would be filled with people who would kiss her hand or her cheek, embrace her, call her by name affectionately, and then begin to talk.

The cab entered Harlem and crisscrossed through narrow streets lined with fetid tenements. On the stoops, even at this hour, were congregations of young Puerto-Ricans, speaking in rapid musical voices, some of them singing softly. At a stoplight a man moved out of the shadows, then darted to the cab window. He wore a wide-brimmed black hat and a light colored jacket with incredible shoulders. He smiled politely and bowed. You want *hombre*, lady? Man?" he asked, making a gesture with his thin hands. "Big one, long like this. Much passion." The offer was made innocently, as if he were selling peanuts from a wagon.

"No, thank you, very much," Carlotta replied, shaking her head.

"Not me lady," the man assured her. "Other fellow. Big like bull. Much big. Much strong."

The traffic light changed to green and the driver stepped on the gas harshly, making the cab leap forward. "This city," he said, over his shoulder. "It's getting to be a regular sewer, New York, with them kind of people. And breed, they breed like rabbits, lady. All of them on home relief, that you and me pay for out of our own pockets."

Carlotta shrugged indifferently and said, "I rather like them. They are a pleasant little people, fond of dancing and light wines."

Stubbornly the driver shook his head. "Where do you live, lady?" he asked. "Park Avenue? Fifth Avenue? What do you know? Nothing. You see what I see, pushing this hack, you would admit that I am right."

He pulled into the curb, stopping in front of the club. The building was dark. The street was dark. A sickening odor of garbage rose from the unswept gutters.

"This the place?" said the driver.

"This is it," said Carlotta. She paid him what the meter read then gave him a five dollar bill. As she leaned forward to hand him the money she saw a heavy monkey wrench on the seat beside him. He touched it, not smiling. "Nobody holds me up," he said. "I'll wrap this wrench around his neck first."

Carlotta got out of the cab and crossed the sidewalk quickly, going down a flight of steps that led to an American basement. The little areaway was dark. There was an iron gate and behind it a steel door with a formidable look. Carlotta touched the bell. A tall Negro in a dinner jacket opened the door and let her in. "Miss McBride, it's a pleasure." He spoke with a West Indian accent and moved like a prize-fighter, leading the way down a narrow hall, through a door with a red velvet curtain, into the club room, which was low-ceilinged and dark as a movie house. There were flickering candles on some of the tables. At the far end of the room logs burned discreetly in a stone fireplace at waist level. There were no windows. Underfoot was a thick rug that deadened the sound. There was a tiny stage and beside it were chairs for three musicians, empty music stands beside them. "Next show in a few minutes," the tall Negro told Carlotta, seating her at a good table. "What can I get you to drink tonight?"

"John Jameson on the rocks," replied Carlotta. "A double, I should think."

When her night-vision came into function she could see the faces around her, white shoulders of women, white shirt fronts of men, haze of cigarette smoke above them. The room was crowded but oddly silent. People seemed not to be talking, or perhaps their voices were killed by the heavy rug and a ceiling made of some rough-textured acoustical tile. They were like a group of people waiting in silence for some catastrophe.

The three-piece combo came through a curtain behind the stage, sat down and made tentative noises. Then a girl in a scarlet dress appeared on the tiny stage. A baby spot came on, lighting her head and shoulders. She was a honey-colored girl with lots of rich black hair. She sang in a low thrilling voice, fake Billie Holliday but pleasant enough for people who had been drinking. She had been working in one of the downtown cabarets until the police picked up her license on some kind of narcotics charge, Carlotta remembered. When she finished her number there was a round of soggy applause. Carlotta signaled to the waiter. "Ask her if she'd like to join me for a drink at the break," she said.

"Certainly, Miss McBride," said the waiter.

When the girl came to the table, Carlotta realized that she was a very handsome creature indeed. Her skin was gold with an underglow of red that was like copper. Indian blood, Carlotta guessed. Her mouth was full and beautifully shaped. "Very kind of you to ask me," she said, when Carlotta asked her to sit down. "It is an honor." Her manner was almost haughty. Was it contempt or simply fierce racial pride? Carlotta did not know. The waiter came. "I'd like a pot of coffee, please," said the girl. Carlotta ordered another whiskey.

"I hope you won't think I'm being presumptuous," Carlotta said, when the waiter had gone. "But after all we are both more or less in the same business. I'd like to help you."

"I could do with some help," the girl admitted. "This trap is beginning to get me down."

"I have a friend in City Hall," said Carlotta. "He might be able to do something for you."

The girl looked at Carlotta with some curiosity. The light of a nearby candle played on her red-gold features, making her teeth look uncannily white. After a moment she said, "Why would you want to take the trouble, Miss McBride? You don't know me."

"I've been in trouble myself," said Carlotta. "I would like to help you."

"It can't do any harm, that's for sure," said the girl. "Three times I've been down to see that little hitler at police headquarters. He just laughs in my face."

She wrote her name and address with lipstick on a paper napkin. Carlotta put the napkin into her bag. What a collection of objects I am acquiring tonight, she thought, looking at the pills and the letter and the eviction notice she had taken from Arthur the Artist. The girl finished her coffee and said, "Almost time for my next turn. Anything special you'd like to hear?"

When she was sober, Carlotta disliked sentimentality but sometimes when she had been drinking the liquor seemed to touch a maudlin strain in her temperament. " 'Across a Crowded Room,'" she said.

"You shall hear it," the girl promised. "And thanks for the coffee."

The two women shook hands. The Negro girl went back to the microphone on the little stage. She bent down and spoke to the musicians, then began to sing the song she had promised Carlotta. In the candlelight, Carlotta wept softly to the words she had heard a hundred times. It was delicious imitation sorrow. She was enjoying herself, alone in the dark, her hands moving moth-like as she raised and lowered her glass to drink.

"I suppose you cry a lot," Doctor Fowler had suggested.

"Never," she had told him firmly. "Except, of course, when I've been drinking. Then sometimes I'm a regular river. But I enjoy that, Doctor. I enjoy it. It's not real crying, you see. It's just stage crying."

When the song was finished Carlotta applauded. The other customers were bored, too sodden to respond to anything but the most insistent music. The girl gave them a lively song that had not been written for the general public: "Daddy-oh, Daddy-oh, I like the way you go, but I can't breathe."

When the music was over the room was filled again with a thick, unnatural silence. Carlotta felt the walls close in. She had the sense that all around her there was malevolent, sinister breathing. She signalled the tall Negro and asked for her bill.

"Shall I get you a taxi, Miss McBride?"

"No thank you, I want some air," Carlotta said.

"You sure now?" he asked doubtfully.

"I'm all right," she said. "I'm going to walk for a bit."

She signed the bill and gave the waiter a good-sized tip. The tall Negro showed her out. "You be careful now, miss, you hear?" he said. "And hurry back."

Carlotta promised to be careful and stepped out into the street. It was seven o'clock, grey dawn, with a trace of pink in the ribbon of sky between the files of tenement buildings. The long sad street was empty. The dirty brownstone fronts of houses looked like a stage-set. There were cars parked along the curbs, old ones mostly, with here and there a glossy Lincoln or Imperial or Cadillac. "No matter how much money he's got a Negro can't rent a decent apartment or go to a first-class resort hotel, so he puts his spare money on his back or into a big shiny car," some-one had told her.

She had no car.

Once she had owned a Jaguar, but someone had borrowed it and wrapped it around a telegraph pole and she had not bothered to buy another.

She walked east toward the river through the long monotonous street, populated only by the occasional homeless cat. She crossed the East River Drive to the promenade on the water side and walked south along the river bank. The air was cool and clear, the morning air of early spring. In the grey-pink light, outlines and edges were sharp. The river was very still and steam rose from the surface of the water. The Triborough Bridge, looming high, looked exciting in the morning light.

Carlotta came to a flight of steps that led to a promenade above the level of the motor road. She climbed it slowly, finding herself on a concrete deck some distance above the water. There were benches here and there and sandboxes for children. To the south was central Manhattan, towers rising miraculously against the pale cool sky. Carlotta paused, leaning against the iron guard-rail, looking at the towers, then at the river, then at the bulk of Welfare Island, autonomous as an anchored warship, with its blocks of prison buildings outlined by plots of grass.

She stood with the gentle breeze on her face. During the last several hours she had taken more than a quart of whiskey. Clinically, she was certainly drunk. If they drew the blood from her veins and measured the alcohol held in the blood, they would insist that she was drunk. If she were obliged to breathe into a rubber bag and her breath were to be broken down into its constituent gases, they would insist that she was drunk. Yet she felt not drunk at all. Her mind was racing. Her knees were steady. She bit into her lower lip and felt the rewarding pain. She took a mirror from her bag and examined her reflection. Her eyes were clear. She laughed softly to herself, remembering the man last night, in his absurd hat, smiling at her through the taxi window. "You want *hombre*, lady? Man?" If only one's demands could be met with such marvelous simplicity. You want *hombre*, lady? You want peace, lady?

She straightened up and began to walk, disturbed now by unhealthy visions, tumbling into her mind unwanted, somehow loosened by the absurd remembered phrase of a pimp.

When she reached Sutton Place she turned away from the river and walked into the city. It was eight o'clock and the sun was bright. Well-dressed people were already abroad, smart-looking young women standing on the fashionable street corners, looking for taxicabs, freshly shaved young men in dark and impeccable suits, purposeful and on the way. Carlotta felt shabby beside them and she flushed with guilt, as if the immaculate men and women were intended to inflict upon her a kind of reprimand. She walked west to Third Avenue and went into Clarke's without any self-debate. An old man with a crooked leg was covering the floor with fresh sawdust, sifting it from a burlap bag, a classic pose, the humble sower. The pungent smell of sawdust mixed with the smell of fresh coffee. The brass behind the bar was polished and the young Irish barkeep was crisp and morning clean.

"I would like a black velvet," said Carlotta.

That was why she was here and not across the street in Sheridan's. Sheridan didn't keep champagne and champagne was what she wanted now, sparkling crisp champagne mixed with rich black stout. There was a small exciting pop as the split of wine was uncorked. Carefully, the bartender mixed the drink in a polished glass. Carlotta drank slowly. When the glass was half empty her lips were numb again. Perhaps I shall sit here all day drinking stout and champagne, she thought idly.

She had a second black velvet and all at once she was quite drunk, dangerously close to the edge of the pit. I must go home, she thought. I must. She had been calm as marble. Now she was terrified. She paid for the drinks and made her way to the door, staggering, unsteady on her feet. A taxi stood at the curb, the driver reading a tabloid. Carlotta sank into the seat, shaking her head, and gave her address carefully. The drive was short, a few blocks. Getting out of the taxi in front of her apartment house, she steadied herself on the doorman's arm, managing to walk through the prim lobby to the elevator door without lurching or staggering. She was filled with shame, scalded by it. With the sleek door closed, the elevator was like an enormous upright casket. Carlotta leaned against the wall, clinging to the bronze hand-rail. I am ill, she said to herself. I am deathly ill. She pressed her doorbell, swaying, catching at the doorknob to steady herself. In a moment Katie was there, leading her into the bedroom. "I am sick, Katie, sick to death," Carlotta said, demanding pity.

"I know," Katie said. "Just hold on to yourself now, miss, while I get your clothes off."

In the bed, under the covers, Carlotta shuddered with fear. Then the warmth enveloped her. She felt her thighs go limp. It was almost as if she were going under a general anesthetic. Katie bent over the bed. "Will you be getting to the theater tonight, miss, do you suppose now?"

"I must," said Carlotta. "You know that I must."

"Then I will call Swanberg for five o'clock," the servant said. Swanberg was Carlotta's masseuse, a big Swede with powerful hands and forearms like those of a man.

"I must go to Paris," Carlotta said.

"You go to sleep," the maid said firmly. She drew the curtains and closed the door. The room was dark and silent as a vault. The warm bed was like a womb. Carlotta yearned for sleep.

Yet she could not sleep. She rose in the dark and called for Doctor Fowler. She sat in the warm bed waiting, but he did not come. "Son-of-a-bitch of a quack!" she said aloud and viciously. "Thirty dollars an hour I pay you. You are supposed to listen to me when I need to be listened to. It is your lousy job. When I go into a restaurant I expect to be served with food. When I go into a barroom I expect to be served with booze. If I went to a male whorehouse I should expect to be served with penis. You are paid to serve your ears. Lend me your ears. Ha, ha! You don't lend anyone anything, do you, Doctor Fowler? Thirty dollars an hour. Fifteen dollars an ear. No charge for waiting time."

She lay back on the pillow, accepting the fact that for a long time there would be no sleep for her. Her eyes were open, gazing at the dark. How many hours had she talked while Doctor Fowler listened? One hundred? Two hundred? It was monstrous. It was absurd. Why did I keep on going, after the first time? I should have known better. I am not engaged ... with love or life or art or sex or Doctor William Thurgood Fowler. I am an idiot but I am not stupid. Why did I go back to that awful room, day after day, week after week?

But she had gone back, every day. She had written her autobiography, or most of it, these last six months, a long journey in a quiet room, a journey that had led her where? To her own sleepless, drunken bed? No further than that? But this is where I began, her soul protested. To travel that distance and get nowhere—it is not fair. It is not fair ....

CHAPTER TWO

LONG JOURNEY IN
A QUIET ROOM

WHAT is your name, please? Doctor Fowler had asked six
months ago when first she sat in his beige office.

—I don't know, she had answered smoothly, intending to
disturb his calm. I call myself Carlotta McBride but it is not my
name. That is one of the secrets a malevolent god apparently
intends to keep from me: my name and the date of my birth and
certain other personal details most people seem to find that it is
reassuring to know.

The doctor's calm was not disturbed. Carlotta McBride, he
wrote on his form. When he had put down her address and the
name of the doctor who had sent her to him, he looked up, took
off his glasses, polished them and smiled.

—Why are you here? he asked casually as if he wanted to
know the time of day.

—Why am I here?

She was angry now, impatient with this professional bland-
ness and with what she took to be his bad acting.

—You have the report from the hospital. I see it there on your
desk. I am a drunk, a rummy, an alcoholic, a booze-fighter, a
lush. I was carried out of a Third Avenue saloon on a stretcher
and taken to Bellevue in an ambulance.

—I understand, he said. But why are you here in this room? What brings you here?

She sat silently for several minutes, unable to answer him. Why have I come? she asked herself. Not because Falkstein insisted on it. I have never been bullied. Never. Not because the fat doctor told me it was a good idea. Not because I wanted to come and not because I believe in this any more than I believe in God. But why have I come? I wonder.

She was ashamed of sitting silent. Out loud she said, I need help, doctor. I have come for help.

That was the right thing to say. He nodded and picked up his pen. You can be helped, he said, with confidence that angered her.

—How? she asked.

—We will talk, he said mildly. At least you will talk and I will listen and together perhaps we can find reasons for things that seem to have no reasons.

—I don't know where to begin, she said, her eyes fixed on the onyx stand that held the doctor's clock and pen.

—Begin where you like, he advised her. At the beginning, if you want to. Or the middle. Wherever you please. It doesn't matter.

—I do not know my own beginning. I told you that, she said. I cannot see my own end. As for the middle, well there was someone, a writer I think, who said that there are no second acts in American lives.

—Well then, perhaps you can remember the first time you were drunk, he suggested. I don't mean the first time you had a drink or two, but the first time you were drunk enough to lose control.

The muscles of her throat had tightened and her mouth had gone dry. She was like an animal that scents fear and looks for it. Then her intelligence argued back: Why not try it? You never can tell.

—Very well, I will talk about it, she said, the tone of her voice becoming lower. I can remember and I will tell you. She bowed her head to avoid looking at the doctor, and went on:

—It was on my birthday, my sixteenth birthday. Of course it wasn't really my birthday because when you get down to it, nobody knows the day I was born. She looked up at him then and laughed. Sounds like the title of a popular song, doesn't it? Nobody knows the day I was born.

—Were you alone when you got drunk? he asked. With friends?

—I was with a man called Michael McBride, she said. He used to be my father.

—Tell me about it, the doctor said.

—Before I could tell you about that I would have to tell you something about him, Carlotta said. And about my mother. And something about myself when I was young and uncorrupted, believing firmly in the good God, still trailing clouds of glory.

Doctor Fowler sat at his desk, patient, even-tempered, as if there were all the time in the world. Carlotta had the impression that he was prepared to sit there until hell froze over, whether she uttered a word or not. It will be easier to talk than to sit here saying nothing, she thought. She took a deep breath, held it, then let it out slowly. After a little she began to talk, surprised at the ease with which words were found. She was talking about herself but she had a sense of detachment from the people and events she described, as if she were reading lines from a play.

My mother, she said.

Odd that I mention her first.

She is a strange and lonely woman. Once I told her I hated her. I don't think it was the right word. I don't want to hate her you see. I want to pity her. But to pity one must understand and I have never understood her. She is remarkably Irish-looking: blue-black hair worn close to the skull, eyes the color of bright blue stones. She wears dark clothes mostly and very simple jewelry.

Her appearance suggests a woman of passion, but there is no passion in her. It is a thing she hates and fears. She looks sometimes like an anguished nun who keeps her vows with pain, sins in her mind and scourges herself, a woman filled with detested lust.

My father was not like that. He was a big careless man, handsome and fearfully Irish, almost defiantly Irish. When he had been drinking he became sentimental as one of those Dublin characters in ULYSSES that Joyce likes to crucify, fiercely Gaelic and patriotic. When there were a dozen drinks in him no one would have believed that he had been born in Brockton, Massachusetts, and gone to Harvard College. He would sing rebel songs and tell me stories of the Irish heroes, things he had heard from his own father. He slipped into a brogue as easily as another man slips into moccasins. He was warm, warm as fire, warm as my mother is cold, and he breathed masculinity, so that there was around him always a kind of masculine aura.

One night I can remember. I must have been nine years old or ten. For some reason I had not slept and I heard him come into the house that night at two o'clock in the morning. I crept downstairs in my bathrobe, holding my breath in the dark as I passed the door to mother's room.

I found him in the kitchen, trying to fix himself a plate of scrambled eggs. He had been to some kind of club dinner and was dressed in evening clothes. He was quite drunk, holding the egg shells aloft in the manner of a short order cook, spilling most of the white.

"Let me do it," I said.

"Thank you, mavourneen," he said.

When he had been drinking he used that word: *mo mhuirnin,* mavourneen, my darling. Mother hated the sound of it.

I cooked the eggs carefully, made toast, and poured out two glasses of milk. We sat down at the kitchen table and ate the food together, then went upstairs to the room that was always called the den. It is a squarish room in the front of the house, paneled in dark walnut. There are books and leather chairs and heavy crimson curtains. Built into one wall is a Capehart record player. The sound comes out of a grille fitted into the paneling, high up near the ceiling.

He turned on the machine and loaded it with a stack of records he had ordered from Dublin, Irish ballads, rebel songs, fierce bloodthirsty things, some of them, others sad pale songs of exile and defeat. He fixed himself a drink then sat in a deep leather chair and took me onto his lap. He let me have a sip from his glass. It was Irish whiskey, strong and smoky. I had been told that it tasted like peat, though I wasn't quite sure what was peat.

We listened to the records in reverent silence until the stack had played itself through, then he turned them over and we listened to the other sides. It was a thing we had done before, though never at two o'clock in the morning. There was a singer with a thin, high voice, thin, but very true. " 'Twas on the Belfast mountains," he sang. "Henry Joy McCracken died on the gallows tree." We were listening to that record. There were tears in my eyes.

Suddenly the music stopped. The needle scraped pathetically. We looked up and there was mother, standing beside the machine, eyes blazing with anger. She wore a long black housecoat and looked like an avenging angel. She must have been twenty-eight or nine. To me she looked old as a witch.

"Must you wake the whole house with your drunken noise?"

She caught my arm and pulled me from his lap.

"Carlotta, you wicked child, why do you encourage him?" she demanded. "Can't you see he's drunk and doesn't know what he's doing?"

"He knows what he's doing," I said. "He is playing his Irish records."

She slapped my face on the cheek, hard. "Upstairs with you at once," she said. "Tomorrow's a school day."

I stood there with my cheek smarting, tears in my eyes, contemplating rebellion. It was the first time in my life anyone had struck me.

"Upstairs!" mother said.

I ran from the room, terrified. Behind me I heard her voice, kept low because of the servants, but savage, filled with hate. When he had been drinking, even a little, she hated him without mercy.

I didn't sleep much that night. The next morning I got up and put on my black lisle stockings and my cotton underwear and my blue serge uniform with a white seal on the left breast, and went downstairs to my breakfast. The dining room smelled of coffee and of fresh orange juice. It was a brilliant sunny day and there were birds in the back yard singing. Daddy was reading the newspaper.

"I've a head like a concertina, mavourneen," he said. "I've a tongue like a button stick. I've a mouth like an old potato and I'm more than a little sick." He made a face and said, "The wages of sin, do you understand? Drink up your orange juice, Carlotta, girl. That will never give you a head."

Mother came down, her hair brushed out, wearing a new silk robe, looking young and quite pretty. We had a pleasant breakfast. No one would have suspected there had been a row the night before. In those days, you couldn't even depend on her hatred for him because she would push it under the rug, as she did that morning, and act as if the three of us were a happy normal Catholic family, apple of Cardinal Spellman's eye. But I tell you, Doctor, we were not that. We definitely were not that.

It was a sick house always and filled with her hate. I try to be fair to her, you see. I reach back, I try to remember, but I cannot recall a time when there was any warmth in the house that he did not bring into it.

It is a big private house on East Sixty-seventh Street. My mother lives there now. It is twenty-two feet wide. I had a whole floor to myself, except for the little hall room where my various nurses slept. They came and went, never staying very long. I used to think they went away because they disliked me, but that wasn't so. I found that out later. My own maid, Katie Galvin, has been with me for years. Of course she is grossly overpaid and she gets my clothes when I'm finished with them and last year I sent her home to Ireland to visit her people. Still she does stay with me and I am a lot more difficult now than I was when I was five or six or seven.

So it wasn't because I was a bad child who could not get along with servants. It was mother who drove my nurses away. She was always afraid they would corrupt me, though how I cannot imagine. I can remember some of the nurses, red-faced innocent Irish girls from the hills of Donegal or the bogs of Connemara.

Then I went to school and didn't have nurses any more but only a maid to clean my room and keep my clothes in order. It was the school I went to for twelve years, Doctor, fashionable and expensive, with silent corridors and beautiful nuns. The big house overlooked the park and inside the life of the school purred like a contented cat.

I was one of the girls who wore silk underpants. The most daring thing you could do at school was to wear silk under-clothes instead of the white cotton drawers that were regulation until you reached the Ninth Grade. When I was eleven I had a pair of silk panties and a limp little bra that looked like water wings made for a very small child. I would put on the panties and bra and stand in front of my full-length mirror, trying to admire the effect but always disappointed because my breasts refused to fill the little cups.

Smooth silk pants, under those blue serge skirts! That and smoking in the rest rooms. Thus did we express rebellion against the benevolent regime of the school, supervised by kindly nuns with soft, civilized voices and pale, well-shaped hands. We were young ladies from the best Catholic families and the fees were high. The big stone house on Fifth Avenue was rich and warm and polished, an elegant Catholic cocoon, undertaking to produce standard, marriageable butterflies, flawless and well-behaved.

The war was going on then in France and in North Africa, and then in the burning streets of London, but the war was remote from that quiet, beautiful house. It was the mad foreigners' war. Killing in itself was wrong. That much was made clear to us by the chaplain, young Father Mulligan, who had played football in Worcester, Mass., at the College of the Holy Cross. He was killed later on in the damp jungle undergrowth on a tiny island south of Japan.

The war meant nothing to us. We were concerned with becoming freshmen, wearing any kind of drawers we liked, going to the carefully chaperoned dances. We were insulated from the crude world where people were poor, badly dressed, driven by such forces as desperation or talent, ambition or the yearning for change. We were protected by the school and by money.

Everyone seemed to have money. There was money and there was religion and there was something described as good Catholic breeding. This involved a low-pitched voice, clothes that were quiet but expensive, subservience to the Catholic male, and a hymen preserved intact to the altar. Enthusiasm was discouraged. It was apt to be noisy and somehow Jewish. Sex was never mentioned except by ourselves, in the washrooms. Even Father Mulligan touched upon it with reluctance, sometimes in his sermons. Presumptively, in that great house that contained a hundred people, everyone was a virgin except old Christy Donovan, the janitor and engineer, who had somehow reared sixteen children on whatever the school paid him for keeping the classrooms clean and grossly overheated.

Summers we went to Maine, to a place we called the Lodge, which had belonged to mother's people, given to her as a wedding present. Mother and I stayed all summer. Daddy came down for a month or six weeks and sometimes for a weekend. He would fly down, a thing that was more unusual and daring then than it would be now. Mother had friends in Maine, Catholic women like herself, a staunch minority group. The little stone church in the village flourished on the summer trade, but mother and her friends complained that it was odd to go to Mass and find the church crowded with other people's servants, a thing that never happened at St. Ignatius Loyola on Park Avenue, or at St. Thomas More on Eighty-ninth Street, where the well-groomed worshippers were people like one's self.

I liked the Lodge. It wasn't on the water because the storms were too dangerous but we kept a station wagon and a man to drive it and it only took ten minutes to get from our house to the bright sandy beach. There were striped umbrellas and tents for undressing, square, medieval tents with pennants on top, like the tents on the battlefield in the moving picture Olivier made of Henry V. I suppose it's the same today. I have not been back for a long time now, but I went there every summer of my life for sixteen years.

Of course I was always an outsider with the crowd on the beach, no matter how much they liked me. Do you know what it means to be an Irish-Catholic in a group of well-born Yankee Protestants? When I was little I sometimes fought with the others on the beach. "White Nigger!" somebody called me. "Nigger with your skin turned inside out!"

When we were a little older, the boys and girls in Maine did not tease me about religion or ask rude questions. They simply became very polite whenever religion was mentioned and looked at me somewhat sadly, as if being a Catholic was rather like being afflicted with an incurable disease. If I went to their houses on a Friday they always arranged to have fish. Once, I remember, at lunch time, everyone else was served meat and I was given a plate of cold canned salmon. "I'm awfully sorry, Carlotta," my little friend apologized later. "My mother just clean forgot about your not being able to eat meat on Fridays." I told her that it was all

44

right. But it wasn't. When I got home from the beach I marched straight into the kitchen. It was empty. I opened the frigidaire and found on a shelf what remained of yesterday's roast beef. I cut off a thick slice and sat on the kitchen floor in my shorts, stuffing the meat into my mouth. When I had swallowed it all, I sat there in front of the open refrigerator, waiting for something to happen to me. After all it was a deliberate defiance of God's command as expressed by His Church. I was a sinner and that was for sure. I don't think I should have been surprised had the Devil himself appeared before me, come right up through the kitchen floor, complete with pitchfork and tail. Nothing happened except that I belched because I had eaten the meat too fast. I wasn't exactly frightened but I was relieved just the same to get to confession. The old priest listened to me, clucking his tongue behind the grille. He gave me ten Hail Marys. It was a prayer I loved. Sometimes when I repeated the words tears would come into my eyes and I would swear to myself that I would never marry, but become a holy nun and be a virgin always.

I suppose the idea presents itself at one time or another to every nice Catholic girl. I think that it occurred to me first the summer I started to menstruate. I was rather early with that, and mother was quite embarrassed.

"Why this is terrible, Carlotta," she said when I told her that I needed a Kotex. "You're not thirteen yet."

"I may not be thirteen but I'm bloody just the same," I said, wanting very much to shock her, if possible to make her blush.

"Carlotta, don't tell anyone," she begged. "Promise you won't tell your friends. It doesn't do to get a reputation for being precocious, you know. And little girls do talk. Surely you wouldn't want any of the boys to know?"

I promised not to tell even my most intimate friends. Mother went to her bedroom and got a Kotex for me. It was a thing to be ashamed of and so for a time I was ashamed. Then once when I wouldn't go swimming a fresh little boy smirked and said,

"Wrong time of the month, huh keed?" A friend of mine slapped his face and afterward all of us girls sat around and talked about it. I discovered that I hadn't been so shockingly early after all, but I didn't argue the point with mother. She is a woman with fixed ideas. Fourteen is the proper age for menstruation in northern climates if a girl has been properly brought up. Of course in hot countries, Spain and Italy and so on, one must make allowances.

Even then I understood that her fear of sex was abnormal. It was a corrosive thing and evil, not related to the priggishness or prudishness of the other lace curtain Irish women. She was like a woman who has been the victim of a mass rape or subjected to unmentionable outrage by uniformed sadists bearing heated iron rods.

Her fear of sex. I felt it full in the face during the summer before the war—the American part of the war, I mean, the summer of 1941. Down in Maine, that summer, my friends of the tennis court and beach were beginning to have dates. Kid dates, you understand, Doctor—movies, midnight swims, hamburger parties on somebody's lawn, sometimes a ride with a boy who had a sixteen-year-old's license and could borrow a car from his father, but never a twosome in the car, always four, usually six. They were the sweetly innocent dates described in the slick magazines.

"You may not go," mother said.

"But it's only a hamburger party," I said. "There will be dozens of kids there and no chance to drift away from the crowd, if that's what you're worried about."

"You may not go out after dark," she said.

"But everyone has dates," I said.

"You are not everyone, Carlotta," she said. "You come from a good Catholic family and our standards are different from those of the Protestants. They must be different. When we marry it is for life. We do not divorce, as they do."

"But everyone has dates," I repeated.

"I was seventeen years old before I was permitted to go to a dance and I was home before ten, let me tell you that," she said.

"But that was a long time ago!" I said desperately.

I suppose I was shrieking because she told me to lower my voice or go to my room at once until my temper had improved.

A few nights later, after dinner, I complained of a headache and went upstairs to my room, leaving mother alone in her chair on the broad screened porch. Using the back staircase, I crept out of the house. The Lodge was set a quarter of a mile back from the paved road. The road leading to it was uphill and the surface was gravel. I ran all the way down, slipping and sliding on the loose pebbles, hoping the others had waited for me.

They were waiting. The car stood at the foot of the hill, a long low Chrysler with the top down, powerful engine purring lazily under the hood. There were six of us. The boy I was with was fifteen and in his second year at Exeter, a clean, scrubbedlooking boy with short blond hair and beautiful teeth. It was a handsome evening. The sea air was cool and chaste. We drove along the coast to a little town that had a kind of amusement park built on a steel pier, over the water. We drank Coke and danced a little and went on the roller-coaster. They were very nice boys with marvelous complexions. The one I had was named Toby and he planned to go to Harvard College, where his father had gone before him. At the foot of our hill he kissed my cheek and offered to walk with me all the way up to the house. I thanked him gravely and said no and started uphill alone in the dark. There was a full moon, or nearly full, pale and clear as an oldfashioned patent lamp with a frosted globe. The stars were brilliant and seemed very close. There was no cloud. When I paused to rest for a moment I could see the bay, silver with moonlight. Beyond the breakwater, a thin pencil smudge in the moonlight, was the ocean itself, interminable and dark. On the other side of the ocean were the burning cities of England. I thought about the war that night because the boys from Exeter and Andover and Choate had been talking about aircraft and the prospect of joining the R.C.A.F. I was filled with a throbbing feminine autonomy. A boy had paid for my bottle of pop and for my ride on the roller-coaster, had kissed my cheek and thanked me and asked if he could see me again. I was almost a woman. It was marvelous. I was aware of an undercurrent of atavistic maternal power, strength mixed with gentleness and compassion. I stood in the soft northern moonlight and touched my breasts with my fingertips, making the soft flesh tingle. Then I raised my arms to the summer sky. I suppose I sighed for the sad world. Then I turned toward the house. Off in the hills in the wild forest a fox barked; I felt no fear. Life was bitter-sweet and enormously to be desired, filled with the promise of thrilling adventure and with ideas of greatness.

I climbed the last rise of the hill. In front of the house stood a car with its motor running. At first I thought it must be Daddy, making one of his surprise visits, then I realized that it was a police car, with a floodlight and siren fitted in the roof. Something has happened to Daddy, I thought, choking with sudden panic. There's been an accident. I ran to the house. In the front hall sat my mother, weeping into a handkerchief. Beside her stood a state policeman, wearing breeches and boots and a pistol, his broadbrimmed hat in his hand. I stood in the doorway, terrified, wondering what had happened. Then mother saw me.

"Carlotta, you wicked girl!" she cried.

The state policeman turned. He was a tall young man, flawless as a movie actor, proud of his dashing uniform. "Well young lady," he said. "You've given your mother quite a scare."

"Where have you been?" demanded mother.

"To the beach," I said, looking her in the eye.

She was too conscious of caste to berate me in front of the policeman but when he had gone there was hysteria in the front room, with the oak doors closed so that the servants could not hear. She thought I had been kidnapped, probably raped, perhaps murdered. The state police had already started a systematic search. I was a wicked, cruel, irresponsible girl. Where had I been?

"To the beach," I said stubbornly.

"Alone? On foot?"

"In a car, with other people," I blurted out. "We went on the roller-coaster. A boy bought me a Coke. Two Cokes."

Mother went rigid as if she had been stabbed with a knife. "Did he touch you?" she demanded. "Did he put his hands on your body?"

"Not exactly my body," I said. "He kissed me on the cheek." I was slapped where I had been kissed. "Go to your room at once," she said. "Instantly, do you understand?"

I went upstairs and undressed, put on my pajamas, and sat on the edge of my narrow bed to wait for the fate that God would bring me. I was a disciplined child, you see, used to obeying orders, not very often breaking the rules. I knew that it was wrong to leave the house without permission and I felt guilt, but against this guilt my own soul rose angrily to inform me that mother was even more wrong than I. I heard her voice in the main hall. She was using the telephone. Is she calling Daddy I wondered, half-wishing it were true, part of me wanting to have him know about my adventure.

She was not calling Daddy but Doctor James Malone, the only Catholic physician in the county, an old man, Irish-born, educated in Cork City. In half an hour he reached the house. I opened my door a crack and heard them whispering in the hallway. "I don't think anything happened," said mother. "She's a well brought up girl, you see. But certainly it's best to be sure."

They came into my pretty room together, the old doctor and my mother. "Good evening, Carlotta," the old man said, putting his worn black bag on the floor.

"I'm not sick," I said rudely, covering my breasts with the blanket. "There is nothing the matter with me."

49

"She's an innocent child, James," Mother assured him. "She knows nothing. Nothing at all."

"I understand that, Mary," the doctor said patiently. "And now if you'll leave us alone for a moment, I'll just have a look at Carlotta then."

He was a decent old man with bright blue innocent eyes. When mother had left the room he smiled and sat on the edge of my bed. "Don't hold this against your mother," he advised. "She's a nervous woman but she means well."

I made no comment. The old man sighed and shook his head.

"I'm not going to examine you," he said. "But promise you won't give me away, will you now, Carlotta? In a thing like this it's best to humor your mother."

Until that instant I had not realized precisely what mother had in her mind or why she had called Doctor Malone. Now I was furious; I felt the blood rise to my cheeks. What I experienced was pure clear hatred. Oh yes, I know that you people insist that love and hate are closely related, different faces of the same coin, etcetera, etcetera. Perhaps. What I felt then had nothing to do with love. It had to do with murder. I lay there in my pretty bed with the old doctor beside me and vindictively I wished that I had been raped by French-Canadian tramps, brought home bloody and substantially ruined, bringing disgrace on her and the house.

The next morning at breakfast, she tried to apologize for having called the doctor.

"You think I am harsh, Carlotta," she said. "You are an innocent girl. You don't understand these things. Men can be beasts when they are aroused. Even the decent ones have the devil in them when their heads are turned. And if they've been drinking there is no pity in them. No pity at all. They are like wild beasts. Animals."

I stared at my plate. The eggs were like bulging yellow eyes, regarding me with contempt. I could not imagine young Toby, who had bought me a Coke, playing the part of a sex-crazed beast. I raised my head, looking at my mother. There were tears in my eyes. "You had no right," I said. "You had no right not to trust me."

"I trust you, believe me," she said. "It's that other thing. It can never be trusted. Your whole life could be ruined. Smashed."

"You had no right," I repeated.

It seemed to me that she was determined to prevent me from grasping at the unwinding thread of my own life, determined to murder my youth, in revenge for something that had injured her, with which I had had nothing to do. She is my mortal enemy, I thought. My own mother, my enemy.

The next weekend Daddy came down from New York and the character of the household changed at once, as if all the doors had been flung wide open after having been closed for a long time. It was a kind of ventilation that he seemed to bring with him.

We went to the beach every day and swam in the bright clean ocean. He was tall and strong, with great muscles and a powerful neck, altogether masculine; so much so that the schoolboys and the other fathers seemed not fully developed. Even the brown young lifeguard on his white tower ceased to be a Greek god when Daddy was on the beach. Instantly, that summer, I was infatuated with him. We were together all the time. During the day we swam and sailed in a little sloop that he had borrowed. At night we had parties on the beach, with a driftwood fire and grilled steaks or lobsters hardly out of the sea. Everyone was invited. Everyone came. They were real parties, much better than the little dates and automobile drives. Mother never came with us. She sat on the porch in her wicker chair, eating her dinner alone when we had gone to the beach.

One night I heard them talking after I had gone to bed. They were on the front porch and I knelt by a window to listen. I could see them in the shadows.

"You behave like a college boy," said mother. "It is disgusting."

"For the love of heaven, Mary, I come up here to relax," he said. "This is the way I relax."

"With a pack of children?" she said. "You are thirty-six years old, Michael, too old to be parading like a peacock, showing off your muscles to a lot of schoolgirls. And you are turning Carlotta's head. You make her think there's nothing to life but having a good time."

"She's a young girl on vacation," he said. "Summer is the time for fun."

"Fun!" she said contemptuously. "She is my daughter, Michael. I will not have her corrupted."

"What would you want her to do, Mary?" he asked gently. "Stay home all day and count her beads?"

"You needn't make fun of religion," she said. "Some things are bigger than you are."

He knelt beside her chair and tried to embrace her. She pushed him away. "You have been drinking again," she said. "I have asked you not to drink here. Don't you get enough of it in New York? And enough of the other thing too?"

"I'm not a bad man, Mary," he said. "I do my best. Why don't you forget the past?"

"I detest you," she said. "And I despise you."

"Hate is a rotten thing to live on," he said.

"It is all I have," she said.

He stood up; I could see his silhouette, black against the moonlight. "We could get a divorce," he said. "Other people do it."

"I am a Roman Catholic," she said with terrible pride. "I am married to you and I will live with you. It is God's will. Perhaps it is His way of punishing me."

"Don't try to convert me," he said. "Remember, Mary, I'm a Catholic too."

"A bad one," she said.

"Perhaps," he said.

I heard the porch door slam. He came into the house and I heard his step on the stairs, then the running of water in his bathroom. I knelt by my window, trembling, my head on the sill. I was frightened. It was the first time I had heard her put her hatred into so many words. And I had listened to the tone of her voice. It terrified me. She hated him in the way a good Catholic is supposed to hate sin or the way a soldier is supposed to hate the enemy—without question or equivocation.

Why? I wondered. What had he done? Why was being married to him a punishment inflicted by God?

I raised my head to the sensual moonlight. It was liquid and rich, almost palpable. I could hear him moving in his bedroom. I loved him desperately. I vowed to the moon and the beautiful night that I would never love anyone else.

That summer we were together all the time. He was not drinking except for a can of beer on the beach or a stiff whiskey at sundown. He had time for me, lots of time. We swam and sailed and took long drives. We adored each other or so it seemed to me. Mother did not interfere. I thought that she had been defeated and I was the arrogant, insufferable victor. I was wrong and she was wrong. I should have been slapped and sent away to do penance in a corner.

We closed the Lodge at the end of summer. I put away my shorts and halters and bright colored beach clothes and tried on my school uniforms. During the summer my figure had changed. Nothing seemed to fit, uniforms or weekend clothes. I tried on the illegal brassiere that had looked like a stricken balloon last spring; the cheap silk cups were tight as drums. I couldn't hook the bra in back. "Mother, I need new clothes," I said. "Put what you've outgrown into a pile," she said. "It will be sent to the Catholic Charities."

We went downtown to shop. At Best's, in the girls' department, the old woman smiled and shook her head. "I'm afraid we've lost Carlotta," she said, touching my cheek affectionately. "You'll have to take her upstairs to the junior department."

"Don't be absurd," said mother. "She's not fourteen."

"It's not altogether a question of age," explained the old saleslady, who had known both of us for years. "It's the shape, you see. Some of them change quicker than others."

Mother refused to go upstairs. In the girls' department I tried on half a dozen dresses but nothing fit. We went home without having bought as much as a skirt. The next day I went back to the store alone and ordered what I needed. I chose the most daring party dresses I could find in what is a rather decorous shop, things that exploited my ripening breasts and my newly prominent derrière. I was certain that mother would pack them up and send them back to the store. I was lucky. She had an attack of migraine and took to her bed for a week. It was Daddy who inspected the dresses and he approved of everything.

The party dresses had been ordered for the autumn dances. They were awful. The dances I mean, not the dresses. The boys were freshmen like ourselves, fourteen years old, our equals in nothing but age. In their dark blue suits and white shirts, they looked exactly like one another. Of course they were not all the same. There were the timid and terrified boys who stepped on the toes of your new slippers, and there were the others who assumed you were afraid of them, insolent contemptuous boys who tried to masturbate themselves against your body while you danced with them, muffin faces innocent, eyes fixed on a steady point, only the hot adolescent breath destroying the clinical composure. It was obscene and ugly, the boy approaching an orgasm, his face innocent as milk, the girl drenched with embarrassment, afraid to make a scene.

In spite of the heavy chaperonage, there was a certain amount of primitive smooching on the refreshment room benches and on the stone balconies that overlooked the park. We girls had a set of rules, thrashed out in the toilets amongst ourselves. A boy could kiss you if you liked him, but you must not allow him to put his tongue into your mouth. He could touch your breasts quickly, pretending it was an accident, but you must not permit him to put his hand inside the bodice of your dress. He could touch your behind in the same way but if he tried to get under your skirts you slapped him and made for the bright lights at once. I remember those kisses on the balcony. It was rather like kissing a sponge rubber ball. We all knew from the movies, of course, that it wasn't the real thing, but it was better than nothing and we did get a sense of feminine power because the boys were so uncomfortable... so crammed full of the sense of sin, ashamed of the hardness in their trousers, devilishly frustrated. Of course there were girls who permitted nothing, not even the antiseptic kisses, and others who encouraged a great deal more. I stuck to the rules. It was what most of us did.

That year my best friend was Mindy Collins, a scholarship girl whose father worked on the New York *Times*. She was earnest, intense, and intelligent and she wanted to be a writer. She was the only girl I knew who wanted to be anything, except to be older. In the afternoons, that autumn, we would ride across the park in the bus to Central Park West, where Mindy lived. It was an old apartment house with a great tiled lobby and elevators driven by shabby Negroes. Always we would be alone in the rambling, old-fashioned apartment. "You mean your mother works too?" I asked incredulously, the first time I went home with Mindy. "Of course," said Mindy. "She has always worked, as far as I know. What else would she do with her time? After all, she could hardly devote herself to the horrid poor. We are too close to them ourselves."

Mindy regarded the rest of us with tolerant amusement. Her parents were indifferent Catholics who had sent her to school with us with the idea that she'd get a better education than what was offered in the public school on the West Side.

The Collins apartment was filled with books. There were books everywhere, even in the bathroom, piled on the floor beside the pot, most of them still in their bright colored wrappers. In our house we had Charles Dickens, Cooper's Works, The Complete Works of Marie Corelli, the Lives of the Saints, and so on, things that were never opened, taken down from the shelves only to be dusted and put away again. In Mindy Collins' house were books that people actually read, novels about men and women who lived in the regular world. "Of course you can borrow," Mindy said. "Only be careful and don't lose. You rich are always careless with other people's property."

Mindy's apartment became a kind of lending library for me. Almost every day I would carry home a modern novel, camouflaged with a paper cover so that it looked like a school book. You can get drunk on reading, I think, just as you can get drunk on whiskey. I read everything I touched:—Hemingway, Joyce, Faulkner, Proust, James M. Cain, Colette. It was that autumn that I decided I wasn't going to a Catholic college, even if I had to scrub floors in order to pay my way elsewhere. It wasn't that I had lost my religion. I still took that for granted. It was simply that I wanted to read, read, read, to read everything that had been written.

We were all at home when the war began. Yes, the radio was turned on. It was exactly like the same scene in a dozen movies. The same baffled announcer's voice, breaking into the program. The same stunned American faces. The same disbelief. The same short masculine curse. "The dirty little yellow bastards!"

Pearl Harbor. The great cliché. The place we remember in song as we remembered the battleship Maine. Or was it the Alamo? Yet it is not quite possible to destroy the reality with typecasting or a jukebox tune. The moment of shock was real. For an instant the war was there, in the very room; one held his breath for a few seconds, half expecting that the bombs might fall.

While the radio was giving the news none of the three of us spoke, except for Daddy's muttered sentence. When the music came back on the air I saw him looking at mother. He was happy. He was smiling. He looked at her as if somehow she had been defeated.

"You are too old, Michael," she said sharply. "War is for boys and young men."

"We'll see about that," he said. Unconsciously, perhaps, he straightened his shoulders, sucked in his stomach, touching it with the tips of his fingers. Then he patted the top of my head and went out of the room, his step springy and quite youthful.

"Will he go?" I asked. "Will he really go?"

"Of course he will go," said mother contemptuously. "Wild horses couldn't stop him going." She hated him, she despised him, yet she resented the idea that he might somehow escape, even at the risk of his life. I know, Doctor Fowler. Love and hate. I know.

In less than a month he was gone, not into the quartermaster corps or the adjutant-general's department, where other businessmen went, but into the infantry as a private soldier. Nowadays we are all familiar with military terminology. In 1942 I didn't know precisely what the word infantry meant so I looked it up in the dictionary:—INFANTRY: soldiers who fight on foot with bayonets, rifles, machine guns, grenades, mortars, etc. derivation: *infante:* youth, foot soldier.

There was a clarity that struck at my heart. I memorized the definition.

Daddy went to a camp in Georgia where he learned to fight on foot with a rifle. It changed him. When he came home at the end of three months he was thinner and harder and actually younger. It was a warm week in April and he wore cotton uniforms, beautifully laundered. We walked together on Fifth

Avenue and the pretty girls smiled at him. He was a real soldier, not simply a civilian who had put on a uniform in order to do the same kind of work he had done when he went to the office.

In our class four other girls had fathers who had gone into the army or navy. All of them were officers of some administrative variety. Daddy was the only enlisted man, an ordinary fighting soldier, who would kill people and who might be killed. Everyone thought it was odd, but only Mindy was blunt about it. "How old is your father?" she asked. I told her that he was thirty-six. "Why is he in the infantry then?" she asked. "He must be a case of arrested development."

It was the end of the friendship and the end of my free library. That didn't matter so much, because I had persuaded Daddy to join the Society Library and there I was allowed to go into the stacks, which were always crowded with non-Catholic girls from Spence and Chapin and Brearley.

Soon he was gone altogether, moving with others toward the sound of the guns. He did not write very much. A postcard sometimes, or a short letter. When he was commissioned he sent me a pair of lieutenant's bars. I have them still.

We were alone then, mother and I, in that big house that must have been planned for a family of six or eight. We were like prison cellmates who detest one another, trying to make the best of things.

I want to be fair, Doctor Fowler. She tried. At least, at first she tried. We had meals together, breakfast and dinner. She asked about school, about the girls I knew. She took me to the theater once and once to the Philharmonic.

It was no use. Without him the meals were dreary. The whole house was empty and dreary. In her own way she must have missed him as much as I. When he was at home she hated him. It gave her something to do. Gone, I suppose she hated him too but the fuel for hate was not there.

I missed him in the way an Eskimo must miss the sun during the winter long night. I kept a picture of him on the work desk in my room, a snapshot someone had made at Fort Benning. He was in cotton khaki, leaning against a fence, laughing at something or other. It was a very appealing photograph. Mother detested it.

"The hero!" she said bitterly. "He joined the army for one reason. To escape his obligations. Suppose we all turned our backs on our responsibilities? Where would the world be then?"

I looked at the photograph. He was smiling; I could hear the sound of his voice. I missed him so much that my heart ached. "I hate you, mother," I said.

She stepped back as though I had struck her.

"Don't say that, Carlotta," she said. "For the love of God, don't say that."

I was a child with a child's cruelty in me. "I hate you mother," I repeated. "And I despise you."

She looked at me, her eyes blank with shock. Then she said very slowly, "I hoped you wouldn't. I hoped and prayed that you wouldn't hate me. But I suppose it is God's will."

She went out of the room.

After that she avoided me. She would have her dinner sent upstairs two or three nights in the week. Soon she was having her breakfast in bed. The household was silent and seemed deserted. I was baffled and lonely.

I would eat dinner by myself or not eat it at all, do my homework, and then read until I fell asleep. A big house, I suppose, can be lonelier than a small one. Weekends, sometimes, I would be alone in the house for hours. Mother would be at church or at some kind of religious meeting. The servants would be gone for the day. I would wander from room to room, able almost to taste the silence. It was the house I had lived in all my life. Still, during my explorations I felt like an intruder and could be startled by the slightest noise, the closing of a car door in the street, the creak of one of the old beams that sometimes sounded like a person on the stairs.

I would go into Daddy's bedroom, haunted by the familiar smell. It was a big dark room on the third floor of the house. The walls were painted a deep cinnamon. There was a good oriental rug and English brass at the fireplace. The windows were heavily curtained to keep out the noise from the street. In the bay window stood a Georgian desk, always beautifully polished. There were leather chairs at the fireplace and the bed was a studio couch, made up to serve as a sofa. On the walls were photographs of clubs and football teams and various individuals, none of whom I knew. It was more like a study than a bedroom and I suppose that is what it had started out to be, when they were first married. There were twin beds in mother's room, handsome reproductions fitted with testers and crisply starched canopies, and there was a second chest of drawers. It was a connubial bedroom, obviously so planned, but I can't remember that he ever slept there.

There were two closets in his room, both filled with his clothes, dozens of handmade suits from Brooks Brothers' custom department. Sometimes I would sit on the floor of his closet, beside the neat parade of shoes, the costly suits hanging above me like some vegetation, choked by the profoundly masculine smells.

I began to enjoy my freedom, especially on weekends. We were dismissed from school at noon on Fridays, to give us time for shopping and the dentist. I would explore the city, sometimes alone, on foot, sometimes with a friend or two. None of us really knew anything about New York beyond the boundaries of the well-to-do, the so-called silk stocking district on the upper East Side in Manhattan, the smart shops—Bergdorf's, Bonwit's—a few restaurants, the quiet streets off Park Avenue. When we went to the theater we went by taxicab or car. We did not wander through the Broadway crowds or observe the flea circus culture that flourishes north of Times Square.

Now I approached the whole city in the mood of a permanent tourist, wanting to see everything. Sometimes I would get on the subway and ride far into the East Bronx, leave the train and walk for hours through the drab, repetitive streets, or cross the bridge to Brooklyn, which only the dead are supposed to know.

We were, in the end, no different from others turned loose in the city. It was the Village that drew us, more than any other part of the town. We found an espresso place on Bleecker Street. This was long before they had become a fad. The coffee was ten cents and the customers were divided between old and moustachioed Italians who played draughts and backgammon and young apprentice bohemians who lived in cold water flats, in those days still to be had cheap. The young men were Four-F's, dressed in jeans and flannel shirts. The girls were mostly actresses of the avant garde, playing at the Cherry Lane and places like that. In those days it was called the "Little Theatre Movement." Nowadays, it's "Off-Broadway." Of course the plays are better now and so are the actresses.

There were always a few predatory Lesbians and we fresh-faced girls attracted their attention. Most of us weren't altogether sure what being a Lesbian meant. In actual, physical terms, I mean. We understood that they were lady-lovers because that was what we called them. They stared at me, in the coffee shop. I was going on fifteen and well-developed for my age. I had always been pretty, in a picture book kind of way, but now I was filling out and the sexual chemistry was at work. People stared at me on the streets and grown men tried to pick me up.

We went out into the city looking for adventure, looking really for trouble, I suppose, as much as the little V-girls who were beginning to infest Times Square, though we were not as honest as they—we didn't admit it. We didn't want money or gonorrhea or a bottle in a cheap hotel room. We wanted excitement that was safe. Our maidenheads were to be preserved intact for the wedding night, so we avoided the soldiers and sailors who wandered through the city by the thousands, sniffing the air like predacious dogs, and we by-passed the college boys in their khakis and naval R.O.T.C. raincoats. We were above all that. We went to Greenwich Village and sat at the feet of the unfit, drinking black bitter coffee, listening to black bitter conversation.

I was curious about the Lesbians. Perhaps that's not the right word. To me they seemed unbearably lonely, cut off, somehow deprived at birth, and in an odd, oblique way they reminded me of my mother. She is lonely and cut off too, and somewhere buried in her loneliness is that hideous sexual fear, that terror of men that has always informed her life and almost stopped her breathing.

During the first winter we went to the Village, I developed a nodding acquaintance with most of the regular customers at the espresso place, except for the old Italians. They ignored me, as they ignored the young bohemians of all four sexes. Sometimes I flirted with the old men, hoping one of them would pinch my cheek or even my bottom and exclaim "Bella! Bella!" the way Italians do in the movies. They were invulnerable, devoted to checkers, to coffee and especially to each other.

There was a dark girl I spoke to, dressed in what later became the ballet dancer's manner—pony tail, dark stockings, thick woolen skirt cut very full, man's denim workshirt, carelessly laundered, wooden jewelry, flat shoes. She wasn't an obvious Lesbian like some of the others, with their cigars and trousers and shaved necks. She called herself Tamara Kent, having evolved this from Tamar Cohen, and she was trying to be a painter, working at the Art Students League and supporting herself precariously by posing for third-rate photographers. One day when the coffee house was crowded she sat down at the table with me. I was alone. She asked permission politely and for several minutes said nothing. She was a timid girl and must have been quite young, twenty, perhaps, or twenty-one. She had a mournful sallow-complected face and very large, defensive eyes, dark-brown and beautiful. They were her only beautiful feature. Her hands were squarish and too big. Her legs had a forthright peasant strength that was not altogether appealing.

We talked about the coffee and then about the weather and then about a book we had both read. She was an earnest girl, serious about life and art and sex. I suppose she was rather stupid, but she was a change from the girls at school. She was Jewish and she was poor and she lived by herself in Greenwich Village.

It was a Friday evening. When we parted I promised to meet her on the following afternoon. I was going through one of those phases when school and everyone in it seemed dull to the point of desperation. I had been struck by the conviction that my life was being used up without my permission. At fifteen it seemed to me that I was dying on the vine. At least my new acquaintance, Tamara, lived according to her own clock and not by a system of school bells. She wore what she pleased every day, not just on the weekend, and probably already had been to bed with someone.

The next day when I woke up it was snowing, nearly a blizzard. I took a taxi and told the driver to stop a block from the espresso place. It seemed inappropriate to arrive there in a taxicab.

Tamara was waiting for me, staring patiently at the sludge that remained in her little cup. She wore a black jersey and an arrangement of wooden beads. When she moved she made a noise like one of those beaded doors they use in summer in the south of France. We drank coffee for an hour and talked. Two old Lesbians, hawk-faced, rapacious, watched us with some interest. Finally Tamara said, "I am an artist, you know. I would like to paint you." "Why?" I asked ingenuously. "Because you are very beautiful," she said reverently. "You are the most beautiful human being I have ever seen."

We walked through the snow to her studio, which was in a tenement building a few blocks away from the espresso place. Italian boys, their strong black hair white with snow, shouted obscene compliments at me, making that rude gesture with the forearm and fist. "Don't be afraid," Tamara said. "They don't mean anything by it." Even at fifteen I knew better than that, but I did not disabuse her.

Tamara's studio was a good-sized room on the top floor of the old building. There was a steep smelly staircase and the mustard-colored walls were filthy. The wooden stair treads creaked as we went up. The studio itself was clean. The walls had been recently white-washed and the wide floorboards painted crimson. There was an easel and a model stand and a taboret smeared with paint. There was a sagging couch with a dark gold corduroy cover and at least a dozen bright colored pillows, small and plump, piled against the stark white wall. Near the bed was a kerosene stove, dangerous but fearfully efficient. The studio seemed intolerably hot after the bitter cold of the street. The room faced north and the whole north wall was window. Daylight sifted through the driving snow, giving the room and the objects in it a poetic, neutral light. It was romantic. I was impressed.

"Of course it's only a sublet," Tamara explained. "It belongs to a friend of mine, a painter. He is in Mexico for the winter."

Since that afternoon I have been in dozens of such rooms. Hundreds, maybe. Always, they have been sublet from the original owner, who is absent in Mexico or Spain or somewhere else where the sun shines and the living is cheap.

Tamara got out a bottle of cheap sherry and a pair of dissimilar jelly glasses. I hesitated. It would be the first time I had taken a drink outside of the house and I remember that the step seemed important. It was sweet sherry and I don't suppose I could drink it now without gagging, but on that Saturday afternoon it tasted good, especially after the second glass. The little stove simmered happily, making the room as warm as an oven. Outside, beyond the window, was the silent inexorable snow. There was that end of the world feeling one gets when it has been snowing for hours and everything is hidden or changed in shape and it is impossible to believe that the snow will ever stop or that it has ever been not snowing. I felt pleasantly drowsy, lulled by the rich sweet wine. I sat on the couch, the bright pillows behind me, watching the snow. Tamara sat on a straight chair, making a charcoal drawing of me. "Have you ever been with a man?" she said, not looking up at me. "Of course not," I said, rather priggishly. "Have you?"

The wine had given her the confidence she had lacked in the coffee house. She laughed and told me that she was not a child. Then she put away her sketch pad and refilled our glasses. She sat beside me on the couch, making the springs creak. "I don't like men," she said. "I don't like their hard bodies. I don't like that hard thing in me. They think they are doing you such a favor, putting themselves inside you." She took my hand and kissed it. "I like you better than any man," she said. "You are soft and beautiful as a flower." She bent over me and kissed my cheek, making her absurd jewelry rattle. I was frightened and faintly disgusted but I was also curious and the wine had been aphrodisiac as well as disarming. This was what we whispered about in the school toilets when we weren't whispering about boys. I closed my eyes, sinking back into the little mountain of pillows. Tamara kissed my mouth and put her hand on my breast. "Open your dress," she said, her voice hoarse and unfamiliar. "Let me see your breasts." I did not move or open my eyes. Awkwardly, she began to unbutton my dress at the top. She kissed my throat, then loosened my bra so that my breasts were exposed. "Let me undress you," she whispered. "I want to see your body."

I did not resist her. I was the non-participant patient, etherized upon a table. I lay there like a statue while she undid the rest of my dress and stripped off my stockings and garter belt and tight silk pants. I have felt this way in a dream, I thought, my mind turning in a haze of sherry. It was not reality. It was like an erotic dream, there in the warm whitewashed room with the snow at the window. Tamara stood up and removed her beads, then took off her shirt and skirt. She wore nothing underneath those two garments. She stood in her dark green stockings, staring at me. Then she was on the bed beside me, I saw the hair under her arms and the blotched skin of her breasts. Her mouth was slack and hideous, like the mouth of an animal one does not care to touch. I rolled away toward the wall and vomited on the bed. I began to cry. Tamara tried to comfort me but I thrust her away. I got up and put on my clothes. I did not offer to clean up the mess I had made on the sheets. The smell was disgusting. "Goodbye," I said. Tamara was crying now. "It doesn't matter," she said, remaining there on the bed, where I had been sick.

I went down the smelly stairs and out into the snow. It was beginning to get dark and the street lights were coming on. There were no taxis. I rode home on the subway in a car crowded with people and wet with melted snow. There was a choking smell of wet wool and a sense of being confined. The sherry hadn't quite worn off and I clung to the strap in the swaying car, feeling sick to my stomach, holding on, determined not to disgrace myself.

When I got home I went straight upstairs and took a long soapy shower, scrubbing myself with a stiff brush until the skin of my body was sore to the touch, as if I could scrub away with soap and water the degrading encounter with Tamara.

I put on a warm woolly bathrobe and went downstairs to have dinner by myself, gnawing through a small steak, ignoring the vegetables. Since it was Saturday I had no homework to prepare for the morning. I went into the kitchen as soon as the cook had departed. There were always half a dozen cans of beer on the racks in the door, kept there by the cook for her own use. I took two cans and an opener and went upstairs to the den. I turned on the Capehart and played through the whole stack of Irish Rebel records, sitting in Daddy's big leather chair, drinking cold beer from the can.

I went back to the espresso place, but never alone again and never again did I go home with Tamara. Mostly I kept to myself. I was reading a great deal and working hard at school, harder than anyone else and harder than was expected or approved. I got the reputation of being queer—moody and intellectual—and there was for a time the rumor that I had forsaken the Catholic Church. It was untrue; the Catholic Church had forsaken me. Since the quarrel with Mindy Collins I had no close friend and I thought of myself as a lone wolf.

Then there was the war. After the landings in Normandy I began to follow the battle news every day in the New York *Times*. Daddy was with the First Division, in command of a rifle company of the Eighteenth Infantry, and I was terrified for him. All through the early days of the invasion I watched the papers and listened to the radio, unable to sleep or to concentrate on anything but the war. It was the bloody battle joined and there was he in the midst of it, crouching in the rain and mud, moving forward with the soaked and bloody mass, perhaps already killed, lying somewhere in an outraged meadow, face turned toward the French sky, eyes wide and sightless, strong hands limp, dead in the mud and the rain. For some reason it seemed to me that it must be always raining where the war was going on; I could not picture waves of soldiers going into the attack beneath a bright warm sun, but only in sullen ceaseless rain, under a low grey sky.

There were no letters. For a long time there had been none, then came a short V-mail note, then for weeks there was nothing. I was certain that he had been killed, or at least seriously wounded. There was the dreadful Christmas of 1944, and the Battle of the Bulge. I was moved to prayer, first at home, beside my bed, then in the great stone church of St. Ignatius Loyola. All around me people were praying, most of them, I should think, praying for some young soldier. All around me the candles flick-ered and the gilt splendor of the altar pieces danced in the shim-mering light. It was no good. Not for an instant did I believe that my prayers or anyone else's could be in any way involved with the bullet or the bayonet or the shell fragment that would kill him if killed he was to be. Never had I been as helpless or hopeless. I felt like one of those people you see in newspaper photographs, held back by police, watching their houses burn to the ground with their wives or children inside them.

Then in mid-winter he was home, without any warning at all.

It was eight o'clock in the evening. I had finished dinner and was getting ready to go upstairs to my homework when he turned the lock with his key and walked into the house. I stopped in my tracks, startled by the sound, then went into the hallway, my heart pounding with fear, certain it was a burglar. There he stood, leaning on a cane, a trench-coat over his arm, heavy army bag at his feet, one of those canvas bags that officers carried. I had changed into a dress after school and put on some lipstick. He had expected a schoolgirl in uniform, with grubby fingers and black stockings and the scrubbed cheeks of innocence. I was a young woman. Literally, for several seconds, he did not recog-nize me. I stood there trembling, wanting to cry out: "It's me! It's me!" Then he dropped the cane. "Carlotta!" He stared at me. "My God in heaven, you're grown up. You're beautiful!" I clung to him, my heart pounding, glad that mother was out of the house and that I had him to myself. She had gone to dinner with one of her friends and then to one of her church meetings.

He picked up his cane and walked into the living room, limping a little. "It's nothing," he said. "In a week I'll throw this thing away." He lifted the cane, an Irish blackthorn that glistened in the light. "It's only a scratch, but it got me thirty days' leave. Or thirty days of what they call rest and recuperation."

I sat on the edge of a straight-backed chair, staring at the medals and the uniform and the prickly Irish cane, not quite able to accept the truth. Then I said, "You must be hungry." Somehow it seemed to be the appropriate thing to say. "That I most certainly am," he said, in his imitation brogue. "I've been living on sandwiches and instant coffee for a couple of days. We came by air, you see. They said it was by way of Iceland, but I'll swear by all the saints that we flew right over the North Pole. And nothing to eat but box lunches."

I rang for the servants. The house was filled with hosannas.

"God bless you, Mr. McBride."

"God bless you sir, may the saints be praised."

He kissed them all on the cheek in turn, the old cook and the young maids. He always had a way with servants. With servants and policemen and cab drivers, head-waiters and people in shops. Somehow they seemed eager to serve him well. I can't remember a cook or a maid who did not worship him.

"He's had no dinner," I told the cook. She was an old woman from Galway, with red cheeks and bright loyal eyes.

"Give me fifteen minutes, your honor, and it will be on the table," she told him, almost kissing his hand.

I mixed a drink for him—Irish whiskey on the rocks—and we sat down to wait until cook was ready. It wasn't until he was halfway through the steak she served him that he said, almost casually, "How is your mother, Carlotta?"

"Mother is all right," I said. I paused before going on, then said, "She goes to church a lot now, and to all kinds of women's meetings."

He nodded and went on eating his dinner. When he had finished and waited for coffee he lit a cigarette and stared at me, seeming really to see me for the first time. "You've changed, Carlotta," he said. "I suppose you have lots of boy friends now?"

I blushed and stammered. "No. Not really," I said. I thought of the adolescent boys who came to our school dances. It was impossible to imagine that any of them would grow up to become men like the man who sat at the table with me, filled with life and warmth. They were neuter, all of them, brash, awkward youths with the guilty eyes of masturbators.

"Ah, they must buzz around you like flies," he said. "You're the prettiest thing I ever set eyes on."

"Do you think so, really?" I said.

"The prettiest thing I've ever seen," he said.

There was no doubt that he meant it; I was dizzy with happiness, ecstatic.

Mother came home at eleven o'clock. We were in the living room. When I heard her key in the lock I stood up and said, "I'd better go upstairs." He shook his head and said, "No, don't go. I'd rather you were here."

He walked to the hallway, not using his stick, limping quite noticeably. Mother stood in the doorway, her hand on the knob, wearing a good black suit and a smart hat. She looked at him, revealing nothing, neither surprise nor pleasure nor resentment, then closed the door behind her.

"Well, Michael, you are home," she said.

"Well, Mary," he said.

"If you'd had the courtesy to let me know you were coming, you should have found me at home to greet you," she said.

"Mary, I'm in the army," he said. "In the army they don't always bother to tell you where you are going or when."

He spoke gently, smiling at her. Then he moved forward, limping, and tried to embrace her. She thrust his arms away.

"Mary, I'm tired," he said. "And I've been wounded."

"If you will go where people are shooting, you must expect to be wounded," she said. She hated the war. It was English and Protestant; she believed in de Valera and the neutrality of Ireland. I felt my throat tighten.

"Mother, you are impossible," I said.

She turned upon me as if she had just noticed that I was there. Her blue eyes glittered in the electric light. "It's past your bed-time," she said. "Upstairs and to bed at once."

I stood there confused, having lost the habit of obeying her.

"Did you hear me, Carlotta?" she said. "Upstairs and to bed at once."

I looked at him as if for advice. There was nothing revealed on his face but pain. He bent to kiss me and I went up the stairs to my room. On the top landing I stopped. Below me I could hear their voices rising hollow in the stairwell.

"Mary, Mary," he was saying. "I thought we could make a new start. Whatever you've had against me, I've changed. We've all changed."

"I have not changed," she said. "You were away and now you are back and that is all there is to it."

There had been a truce in the house. Now the war had started again. I leaned on the varnished banister, not knowing whether I was pleased or frightened. Then I went into my bedroom and got undressed in the dark. At least he is home, I thought. He is home and he is safe.

While he had been away, Mother had steeped herself in religion and illness. It was a climate that suited her. She is a Catholic spinster at heart, the well-to-do old maid who is the delight of the parish priest, always ready to make donations and serve on committees.

She had made a kind of world for herself these last three years; now that world was spoilt by a big man in uniform, smelling of whiskey and tobacco, disturbing the church-like quiet of the house with his singing and his phonograph records, and by a developing girl whose youth must have been a kind of accusation to her.

I don't know what went on between them during the first few days he was home. I know that he tried to please her, joking with her, flattering her, bringing her great bouquets of flowers. One night he went to her room; I heard her send him away. It was hopeless. She had told him the truth on the night of his return. She had not changed.

But he had changed. Before the war he had catered to her, almost been afraid of her, especially if he had been drinking. Now there was a new autonomy in him. When she glared at him if he mixed a drink, he did not put the bottle away. He went right on pouring, had the drink and another, if that was what he wanted. Once, when he was playing his records, she turned off the machine. He got up, using his cane, and turned it on again, smiling at her, saying nothing.

Against this new strain in him she had no real weapon except illness. Two days after he came home she took to her bed. She is a rich woman. Over the years she had acquired a stable of good honest Catholic doctors who saw no harm in humoring her hypochondriac whims. There were nurses around the clock, various physicians called out in the night, dozens of visiting priests and nuns, flowers and fruit from friends. The house was turned into a nursing home and it would have been bad taste had we tried to enjoy ourselves in the presence of such suffering.

It was the week before my birthday. After dinner, Daddy and I sat in the living room with our coffee, the radio turned on low, playing innocuous music. He poured himself a brandy, drank it and poured another. He had been drinking quite a lot these last ten days, not going out of the house, but sitting in the den with a bottle until three or four in the morning, then sleeping until noon the next day. It was getting on his nerves and I could see that he was fighting against a real outburst.

"This house is like a morgue," he said, gulping the second brandy. "We can't stay here, mavourneen, you and I. We're not sick, God damn it. We're well. There's no reason why we should have to live in a God damned hospital."

He had been in combat for two years and gone with the First Division from North Africa to the Rhine. Underneath the control, his nerves were like live electric wires, short-circuited easily by any sudden movement. He reached for the brandy decanter and sat holding it in his hand, not pouring. He seemed to calm himself by means of intense physical effort. It was like watching a man lift an incredible weight. Then he said quietly, pouring the brandy, "She isn't really sick, you know. There's nothing the matter with her at all, on the physical side, that is." He drank the brandy. "I can't stand it," he said. "Before the war, well, I was stronger, maybe. I could put up with anything. Now I can't stand it."

He sat for a long time, brooding, holding the empty glass in his hand, staring at it as if it were a crystal ball that would tell him what to do. Then he raised his head and said, "Let's get into the car right now and drive to Maine. We can open the Lodge. It's too early in the year for Maine, but that doesn't matter. At least we'll get out of this stinking house for a few days."

"What about school?" I said, not knowing what else to say.

"I'll call the school and tell them you're sick," he said. He looked at me, then said, almost rudely, "Don't you want to go? Don't you want to get the hell out of here?"

"Yes," I said. "I want to go."

In less than an hour we were on the way, sitting in the big warm Cadillac, driving fast over the parkway. "They gave me a wad of gasoline coupons," he said happily. "I almost gave them away. I didn't think I'd have any use for them."

He was a superb driver and he enjoyed handling a big powerful car. He drove fast that night, seventy, eighty miles an hour on the straightaway. It was too fast but somehow it did not seem dangerous at all. The car seemed to hug the road, cutting through the night, and there was almost no traffic. The radio was turned on low, bringing in the music of a sweet band playing for the after dinner crowd in some hotel. He hummed and sang along with the music, eyes always on the road. He was the same man I had all my life adored and yet there was something different about him, a quality of recklessness and impatience that came from having been for a long time a soldier who fights on foot, with a rifle, grenade and bayonet. Sitting beside him, watching him drive, it was not difficult to imagine what I could not have imagined before—the blunt fact of his killing people, perhaps even with his own hands.

As we drove through the clear starlit night, behind the powerful engine, he was the only man alive, the only human being alive on this earth besides myself, Carlotta McBride, the Irish Beauty, virgin and schoolgirl, sweet sixteen, kissed in passion by nobody except a Lesbian girl in the Village.

We drove fast through the night and morning and reached the Lodge before noontime. The windows were boarded up and the storm doors had been fitted. The house looked forsaken; I had never seen it that way before. Always when we came in the summer things had been made ready for us. Even our clothes had been shaken out and neatly hung in the closets. Now it looked almost forbidding. There had been a light snowfall and patches remained on the ground. I had a sudden spasm of fear.

"Let's not call Mrs. Blodgett," he said, when we were in the house. "It will be more fun to cook for ourselves and we don't have to make the beds if we don't feel like it. We can just pig in as we pigged out, as my sainted mother used to say when she was too tired to make our beds."

Mrs. Blodgett was the local woman who came in to cook and serve and clean when the Lodge was used off-season and there were no regular servants. She was a dried up Yankee woman, suspicious of all New Yorkers, contemptuous of Roman Catholics. I was glad she wasn't to come.

"Fix me a drink, will you, Carlotta, and make some coffee for us, while I'm getting a fire started," he said, bending over the copper scoop that held a dozen logs of wood.

I went into the kitchen. It was closed up and smelled musty. I plugged in the frigidaire and the motor started. Then I made a pot of coffee and looked around for the whiskey. "There's no ice," I called to him. He drank a stiff drink straight and poured another. I went back to the kitchen and opened a tinned ham.

There was always plenty of food at the Lodge and plenty of liquor too. He liked to be able to drive up on the spur of the moment, just as we had done, and he didn't like to be bothered by stopping en route to shop for food. He was a man who did not like petty complications, in business or in his personal life. He wanted things to be straightforward—cards-on-the-table, gentlemen-don't-tell-lies, honor-is-expressed-by-courage—and there he was, back from the war, cursed with mother and with me, dishonest, elliptical women, playing a subterranean game where the only rule was cheating and gouging in the clinches. Mother's illness was a fraud. So was my schoolgirl innocence. I was alert with sexuality and no more to be trusted than a homemade bomb. He was a simple warrior and no match for his womenfolk, especially when he had been drinking.

You think I make excuses for him, don't you, Doctor Fowler?

Of course it is true. I am trying to arrange the lighting so that he will appear to his best advantage. Why should I not? It was not his fault but mine. I was a Catholic schoolgirl. If I knew nothing else I knew that the membrane between my legs was there to be defended from anyone on this earth and with my life if it came to that.

It was snowing on my birthday, one of those late blizzards you sometimes get in Maine. It had started during the night. We woke up and looked out of the windows and saw the snow driving in from the north, the drifts piling up, then went back to bed. It was past noon when we got up. I cooked lunch and served it, sulking because it was my birthday and I thought that he had forgotten it. I was the one who had forgotten. It was an old game that he played at Christmas and on my birthday, pretending to have forgotten, then roaring with laughter, delighted with himself, when he decided the torture had gone far enough and produced the presents.

This time he did not drag it out in the way he had done when I was little. When we were halfway through our lunch he laughed at me, then took a package from his pocket and handed it to me across the table.

"I guess that's the end of that game," he said. "I suppose you've outgrown it, now that you're sixteen."

I was crying. My fingers trembled. Finally I got the wrapping off. It was a long slender leather box from Tiffany's, blue, with a satin lining, and it held a strand of pearls with a diamond clasp. It was the kind of thing a man will give to his wife or mistress. They were not the chaste pearls that are given to sixteen-year-olds. I went on crying, the necklace in my hands, hardly able to see it through my tears. Then I got up and went around the table to kiss him.

"Happy birthday," he said. "And be damned to the war and the army and the rest of the god damned world." As I bent to kiss him I smelled the liquor on his breath; he must have had a drink or two while I was busy in the kitchen.

I sat down at my place again and we went on eating. He grinned at me, across the table, and said, "Sure you don't mind being up here with me in the woods instead of back in New York?" I shook my head. He clapped his hands together, struck by a sudden idea. "There's champagne in the house," he said. "Enough of it to float a battleship. And we are going to drink it to celebrate the day."

Outside there was a full dress New England blizzard. Inside the house it was warm. There was a big log fire. The radio was turned on. Both of us had sharp awareness that we were cut off from the rest of the world. The phone lines were down. The road was blocked. Only the radio made a bridge to the world and it was a one-way bridge.

I changed into a party dress. I can remember that moment. I stood in my room, wearing nothing but my brassiere, holding my pants in my hand, looking at the snow that drove hard against the windows. I remember putting the pants on, then taking them off again and throwing them into a corner of the room. I slipped the dress over my head, nothing under it but the bra. I remember that dress. It was from Bergdorf-Good-man's and had cost a hundred dollars. It was the most expensive dress I had ever had. It was a metallic fabric, gold, and it had what was later called a plunging neckline. I had gold shoes to go with it and very pale sheer stockings. When I was dressed I put on the pearls and looked at myself in the mirror. I was beautiful and I was not a child.

When I came downstairs the wine was cooling in silver buckets, four of them, each filled with ice and snow, holding a bottle of champagne, the blunt strong bottle necks covered with gold foil. "Four more in the ice-box," he said cheerfully, unfastening the wire on one of the bottles, working at the cork with his fingers. The little explosion startled me and I jumped. He laughed and handed me a glass filled with the marvelous bubbling wine. He was already a little drunk and the reckless mood was on him. "In France you can buy loose champagne," he said absently, looking at the bubbles in his glass. "They keep a bottle under the bar. Coupe champagne."

We linked arms and drank; the bubbles went up my nose.

"Happy birthday," he said. He kissed my cheek and poured more wine, then looked critically at the pearls and said, "They are right for you. They are just right They are beautiful, and so are you."

We drank three or four bottles of champagne. I don't remember. I do remember holding one of the blunt thick corks in my hand, fascinated by the suggestiveness of the gilt knob on top. I was quite drunk, but champagne is a marvelous thing. Some of my perceptions were very clear and I was not in the least sick, as I had been after drinking two glasses of Tamara's cheap warm sherry.

He was drunk too, of course, in an intense, almost frightening way. He sat in a big chair pulled up close to the fire, drinking champagne and talking about the war in the soldier's disenchanted manner, speaking of death and of comrades gone with precision and terrifying detachment. He was not a literary man, and though he always told a story well he had never in the past brought things to life as he did now, talking to me about the war. I sat in the chair that matched his, hypnotized, frightened a little, sometimes crying. The fire burned steadily. Outside, the slant of snow cut off the view from the windows as if they were hung with white curtains. From far off, very low, under his voice, came the music of the radio. The sense of isolation was absolute. We were like people in a film, cut off in the high Himalayas.

The radio program changed. Dance music came on the air, a good band that played with an insinuating rhythm, so that my foot began to move in time with the beat. "Would you like to dance?" he said. I nodded and stood up, already aware, I think, that I moved into a climate of danger and that it attracted me more than anything in all my life had attracted me light and sure of himself, and it was the first time I had been tall enough to dance properly with him. The champagne we'd before this moment. We moved together across the rug, then out to a space where the floor was clear. He was a good dancer, had to drink gave us the illusion that we were dancing superbly. Perhaps we were. We moved slowly to the music, close together, our cheeks touching. Then our bodies were pressed together, thighs touching. Still moving to the time of the music, we kissed. My lips parted. I felt his beard against my skin. His hand that held mine was trembling slightly. I took his cheeks in my hands and looked into his eyes boldly, then kissed him on the mouth. A little later it happened and I had wanted it to happen. I remember the look of shock as he touched me and realized that I was naked, underneath the gold dress. Would he have stopped I wonder, if I had put on my pants? His hand stopped for a moment, then moved again, and then it was too late to stop.

A long couch faced the fire and I was on it and my skirts were up and the raw bare flesh was there pleading to be taken. I felt the sharp jerking movement as he wrenched at his belt and trouser buttons and then at last he was in me. There was pain and a sense of triumph. I felt the convulsion of his body and the odd cry, only half joy, the other half somehow related to the agony of death. Then he drew away from me, shaking his head like a fighting bull that has been mortally wounded. I touched his cheek and drew his head to my breast, stroking his cheek. "It's all right," I whispered. "It doesn't matter. It's all right."

After a long while he got up, awkwardly fixing his clothes. He went to the bar and poured himself a stiff drink of whiskey. "May I have one too?" I asked.

He hesitated, then poured a second glass. How could he have refused?

The whiskey made me warm inside. It was the first real drink of whiskey I had ever had. He sat in a straight chair, staring at me, whiskey glass in his hand. Then he turned and threw the glass into the fireplace. It smashed into hundreds of little pieces. "I don't know what happened," he said. "I must have gone out of my mind." He hesitated, looking at his hands, then at the glittering shards of glass on the fieldstone hearth. "It's the booze," he said, hating it. "The dirty rotten stinking booze."

"It was my fault," I said quietly, wanting it to be my fault, all of it, from the beginning, wanting to take the skein of guilt from his heart, not wanting to allow him to blame what had happened on the whiskey. "It was my fault," I repeated. "I made it happen. It was my fault." I felt the blood on my thighs. "Would you mind going out of the room for a minute?" I said.

He went into the kitchen, his big shoulders sagging. I got up from the couch, holding my skirt, and went to my bedroom. There was blood on my legs and the dress was ruined. I stared at the blood, fascinated, and then began to cry. After a while I stopped crying and washed myself, then changed into a shirt and blue jeans. I rolled the dress into a ball and hid it in my closet. It was the only time I had worn it. I went to the mirror and looked at myself. The pearls were still around my neck and they looked odd with the denim shirt but I did not take them off. My lips were bruised and my cheeks were red where his beard had scraped the skin ... I looked steadily at my reflection, then said, as if I spoke to a stranger, "I am no longer a virgin, you know." My reflection did not answer, but stared back at me from the glass, lips bruised, cheeks rubbed red by the whiskers of a man.

I went back into the living room and called to him. He came through the kitchen door, a jelly glass filled with whiskey in his hand, staggering just a little. He had combed his hair and fixed his clothing. He sat in a straight-backed chair and tossed off the whiskey, an ugly, frightening gesture, a classical, drunkard's gesture, the head jerked quickly back, the shudder, the backhand wipe of the mouth. "I am a son of a bitch," he said. "A dirty rotten son of a bitch."

"No," I said.

He went on drinking through the afternoon. He must have finished the better part of a bottle of Irish whiskey. By early evening he was very drunk, his voice thick, his hands moving uncertainly. But his mind was oddly clear. "Carlotta," he said suddenly. I looked at him, startled by the sharpness of his tone. "Sit down," he said. I had been filling the ice bucket. Now I sat facing him in one of the big easy chairs by the fireplace. "I've got to tell you something," he said. "I don't know whether it will make things better or make them worse, but I've got to tell you." He looked at me and began to cry. Then he looked at the floor, and then up at me again. "I'm not really your father," he said. "You were adopted."

"I don't believe it!" I said, feeling a spasm of fear that ran through my blood like electric shock.

"It is true," he said, and I knew that it was. "We weren't ever going to tell you, but after what happened I don't know. Maybe it's better."

"But we look alike, you and I," I said, grasping at something. "Everyone says so."

He knelt on the floor beside my chair and took my hands in his own. "Carlotta, I'm sorry," he said. "What I've told you is God's truth."

I cried on his shoulder for a long time. Then I straightened up. The first shock had passed. I had absorbed the simple fact and I moved into an area through which I have wandered ever since that afternoon. I was fanatically curious about myself, my identity, that had just been taken away from me by the one human being that I loved on the face of this earth.

"Who were my parents then?" I asked.

He stood up, took a step, then faced the fire, his back to me. "We don't know," he said.

"Why was I adopted?" I asked. "Is there something the matter with mother?"

"It wasn't your mother, it was me," he said. "It is a joke, isn't it? Mike McBride, the he-man, who couldn't make his own children."

I sat up in my chair, my thighs stiff, struck by a curiously practical thought. There would be no complications. Nothing had happened inside my body to start that hideous reward offered to women who receive men into themselves. The pragmatic morality of the female is well known. Books, I suppose, have been written about it. I felt it then, a flooding sense of relief and a perverse insistence that since I could not be pregnant, nothing had really happened.

He sat down in the big chair and began to cry. "Michael, don't," I said. It was the first time I had called him by his Christian name. He did not seem to notice. "Don't, Michael," I said. "Don't cry." He did stop after a while, and wiped his face with a khaki handkerchief. I stood up, tucking in my shirt and rolling up the sleeves, feeling competent and very young. "I will get supper," I told him.

"That will be fine," he said. Already, he had moved to the little bar and was busy with a fresh bottle of whiskey.

I went into the kitchen and began to prepare the meal.

You, Doctor Fowler, have never been drunk. I will make book on that, as Falkstein would say. Oh I am sure you have been tiddly at various medical conventions and perhaps on your wedding anniversary you have gotten mulled to celebrate the day. I mean really drunk. How can you understand what it means to cross over, to leave reality and enter a world where the rules are gone, except for the single and great rule, that one must go on drinking?

That is what happened to us. Sober, I think that one of us would have pulled back from that kiss, while we were dancing. It would have been a thing to remember in secret, making one flinch in his dreams and cry out, but no more than that, an intimation. Drunk, he had no control. Drunk, I took what I wanted, not just the suggestion of it to which perhaps I was entitled, but all of it, all of it.

There was the snow outside and inside there was the fire and the wooden cases filled with whiskey. When we finished dinner he went to the window and looked out at the snow, as if he contemplated plunging through the glass. Then he turned back into the room.

"It was like this in the Ardennes," he said. "In the forest where I was wounded."

He opened a fresh bottle of whiskey and sat in the chair in front of the fire, staring at the slow flame. When I poured a drink for myself he did not protest. "I did not like the Ardennes, but I liked France," he said. He looked at me. There was firelight on our faces. "I wish that I had gone to France when I was young," he said. "It would have made a difference to me, you see."

He was tired. He was exhausted by the war and by his life. I felt almost like a mother to him. I crossed the room and sat on his lap. He held me and we drank together. "Ah Carlotta," he said. "Carlotta."

We stayed at the Lodge for four days, while the blizzard ran its course. I have often wondered what I would be like had we fled the scene of the crime at once and fled each other, appropriately filled with guilt. I don't know. It is not what we did. We stayed at the Lodge those four days and we stayed together.

His defences seemed to collapse. Mine had never been erected. We drank Irish whiskey together and slept in the big bed in the master bedroom. We were not once sober during those four days and very quickly we became absolutely without shame. There is a phrase: "to revel in sin." That is what I did. He would rise naked from the big bed and use the john that served the room, leaving the door open, standing there stark naked, the raw bullet wound on his leg angry and red. He would urinate while I watched, fascinated by the authority of the sound he made and by the absolutely masculine quality of the whole performance. Then he would shake himself and come back to the bed to kiss me and we would make the two-backed beast, alone in that silent house, with the snow piled high at the doors and windows. Then we would drink and drink and drink. We cared for nothing. It was as if a dam had broken, releasing waters held too long.

Shame?

While I was close to him, with alcohol in his blood and in mine, when I tasted his flesh with my lips, felt the bite of his beard on my skin, I had no sense of shame. I was drunk enough with liquor and love and the bright new joys of sexuality to feel no shame at all.

It was not until the morning we left the Lodge that I felt terror. Not shame precisely, but fear that I would be found out by God or by someone else. I was sick from the drinking too. I stood in my bedroom after I had packed, forcing myself to utter the word. "Incest," I said out loud, looking into the mirror, astonished that my face betrayed nothing more important than fatigue. It was the face of a girl, a young woman, who might have been up three nights running, studying for final examinations. Nothing more. There was no scarlet stain, no mark of sin on my forehead. "Incest," I repeated. What is it called then?

A crime against nature? No, that was something else. Then in a blinding flash it struck me that he was not my father. It was not incest then. What was it? Fornication? Adultery? I bowed my head before the mirror, trying to make an act of contrition. The words would not come to my lips or to my mind. "O my God…" I began. I stopped. I was not sorry heartily or otherwise. I was afraid but I was not sorry.

"I am not going back to the house," he said, when at last we were in the car and headed toward New York. "I think now that maybe I should not have come back at all."

I was afraid then and ashamed, with the car pointed toward home. I did not argue with him. I had never been drunk before and now that I had stopped drinking I was ill. We had to pause by the side of the road while I got out to be sick. I felt better then and the fresh air cleared my head.

We drove through the bright clean morning, not speaking for a long time. Then he said, his eyes on the road, "Promise me one thing, Carlotta. Promise you won't say a thing to your mother about what happened or about what I told you."

"I can't go on living with her after what has happened," I said. "I can't."

"You must," he said. "Carlotta, you must."

He left me in front of the house in Sixty-seventh Street. I have not seen him since that day. I watched the car drive off, then went into the house against my will, not knowing where else I could go.

Mother met me in the hall. She said nothing. We faced each other, woman and girl. I think she could smell the stale liquor on my breath. Then she slapped me on the cheek with her open hand. I stood there waiting for her to hit me again, hoping, almost, that she would kill me. She did not. "Get out of my sight, Carlotta," she said. "Get out of my sight."

I was alone with mother again. What she guessed I cannot know. I don't think she suspected the truth, but drinking was bad enough. She said nothing to me after the slap in the hallway. I said nothing to her. We lived in the house as two strangers, I with my two secrets, she with her hate.

We were strangers and now in an odd conclusive sense I was a stranger to myself.

Search for identity.

It is a modern cliché, is it not, Doctor Fowler? Stock in trade of the novelist, the playwright, the advanced thinker. But this is only a game, this search for the real me that goes on in books and plays and on the couches of analysts. Suppose the search is a real one? That I presume would be bad plotting. But it is what happened to me.

When we came back from the Lodge I had been stripped of my identity. I was anonymous. The other thing, the incest or whatever it was, did not trouble me then, except sometimes in the middle of the night or sometimes at Mass when I would be overtaken with a yearning to believe in something, if only in sin. I suppose this shocks you. Even you Freudians must be shocked sometimes. Nevertheless, it is trae. I had no sense of guilt then. That came later and for another reason. The facts that faced me were simple and I have a logical mind. I had been a virgin. I was a virgin no longer. That was a problem for the confessional.

I lied to my confessor, of course. The truth would have been embarrassing. I told him I had been seduced while drunk by a college boy on a weekend date. I remember that I made him a Yale boy and a Protestant.

Why did I make a false confession rather than no confession at all? One forms habits. In those days I was in the habit of making my confession. But O my God! I was certainly not heartily sorry for my sins. I hope they offend Thee Who art so indifferent.

In school that year we studied the Mendelian Theory. After all he was a monk and so his theories must be blessed by God. Genes. Blue jeans and chromosomes. I remember the countless drawings made on tracing paper, copied out of the biology text that had been vetted at Notre Dame. There was Mendel. There were the genes and the chromosomes. I had been Carlotta McBride, only daughter of Michael Martin Francis McBride and of his never-loving wife, the former Mary Louisa Theresa Costain. On Long Island there were grandparents, one each, maternal, rich, Irish, Catholic and proud. Grandpa was a Knight of St. Ovary or some such saint I had never heard of. Once I played with his Papal sword, the gilt hilt rich with crosses and bright fake jewels. When he was not being a Papal knight, Grandpa was the boss of a stevedoring company that, with the aid of Joseph Ryan, may he rest in peace, and various former inhabitants of Sing Sing and Dannemora, seemed to control nearly all of the loading and unloading of ships that went on in New York and New Jersey.

In Brockton on the road to Boston are the simple graves of the McBrides, South Boston Irish who rose only a notch in the world of New England but who sent their sons to Harvard. They were dead before I was born. I never saw them but I saw their graves and the photographs that Daddy kept … squarefaced Irish they were, characters from a play by Synge, people from the West Coast of Ireland, from Sligo Town that faces the sea, where the young girls opened their white arms to the Spanish sailors who swam ashore from the wrecked Armada, giving the world the black Irish, with their jet black hair and their bright blue eyes and their marvelous manners with women. Of course it's not really true, except for a little bit, but it is romantic just the same.

But there I had been, Carlotta McBride, until that afternoon in Maine possessed of a name and of ancestors. Behind the graves in Brockton and behind the Papal nobility were the genes and chromosomes of the generations, back to the kings and bandits in the wild hills of Donegal and the plains of Royal Meath.

I was Carlotta McBride.

Then suddenly I was not.

I had been Irish, Catholic and rich. Now I was merely rich.

I had been an individual with an identity certified by the past and the present. Now I was simply a question mark, a stateless person in the universe of the soul.

I would sit by the window in my room and stare at the people in the street below, wondering if one of them might be my father or my mother—the milkman, the garbageman, the middle-aged policeman, the fat cook across the street, one of the nuns who passed in pairs, gliding leglessly toward some duty. Who were they? Where were they? Where were the people who had produced me with their genes and chromosomes? With his etcetera and her etcetera, in passion, one presumed, perhaps even in love, and then, when the fun was over and the etceteras had been drawn apart, had vanished and taken with them the ancestry that belonged to me as much as it belonged to them.

"The birth of children is the death of parents."

That is Hegel, Doctor Fowler. I had a good non-Catholic education too. The death of parents! Not for them! They fooled old Hegel and they fooled me. Make the two-backedy beast and throw the outcome into the gutter. Cut and run. Shoot the moon. Take it on the lam, pal. Get out of town before it's tooooo late.

They had left me, in the gutter or elsewhere, and now he had left me too. He went back to the war to be wounded again but he did not write to me. I missed him. I wanted him in the most elemental way in which a woman can want a man and for a long time my narrow bed was a place of torture.

I tossed and turned in the night, ripped off my night clothes and hurled them at the wall. I tried what people always try. I made love to my own body in that room of mine high up above the street, coaxing myself, caressing myself, even clawing at myself with my sharp and polished nails. It was never any good. "Shit! Shit! Shit!" I would cry to the ceiling of my bedroom, frustrated almost to madness, unable to coax myself or stroke myself or scourge myself into climactic relief.

It passed.

There is a curious strength in me that comes from I know not where—a fierce will to live, a determination not to be smashed and not to smash myself. I have it now, I suppose, and that is what really brings me here, not Falkstein's foolish demand that I get treatment if I wanted the part. I had it then, in my seventeenth year, a toughness that came to my rescue and that has come to my rescue ever since. Which is why I am here, paying you thirty dollars an hour, and on the stage every night downtown, instead of being in the gutter or in my grave. Sometime I suppose it will fail me, my toughness, my will to resist, and then I will no longer be actress or alcoholic or patient. I will be dead and buried and all the hell and the shame of my life shoveled into the damp hole with me.

CHAPTER THREE

THE LITTLE FORMLESS FEARS

FOWLER, Carlotta thought. Fowler and his fat white pills. It is not playing the game. He is supposed to help me to help myself in my own mind, not by giving me pills that will make me sick or kill me.

She was on the massage table, blinders shielding her eyes from the light, arms limp at her sides. Swanberg's strong fingers brought the blood back into circulation again. Swanberg was a good masseuse, smelling of starch and witch-hazel, looking, in her white uniform, like a dependable Swedish nursemaid. On the folding massage table Carlotta could feel the warm life return to the muscles of her thighs as Swanberg kneaded them. Then Swanberg's powerful thumbs were on her forehead and temples, smoothing away the stiffness that made Carlotta's head and neck feel as if they were carved from wood. With a sudden movement Swanberg twisted Carlotta's head; the throbbing stopped. The wooden feeling was gone. Carlotta sat up on the table, a towel over her mid-section.

"I think I am going to live," she said.

Swanberg laughed and said, "Too much schnapps, no? It gives always the heeber-jeebers."

"Heebie-jeebies," Carlotta said absently, getting down from the table.

"*Ja,* dot's right, heeber-jeebers," Swanberg said agreeably.

"Katie will give you your money," Carlotta told her. "And thanks for saving my life."

She went into the bathroom and turned on the shower. The warm water felt good. Then she turned on the needle spray and the ice cold water finished the job of waking her up that Swanberg had started on the massage table. Thank God for that Swede, Carlotta thought. She is a genius.

When she had rubbed herself down with a rough towel she felt almost normal—except for a trace of queasiness in her stomach. I should be all right, she said to herself. One night's drinking. That is nothing. Nothing at all. Men do that all the time and show up at their office desks in the morning. Her stomach turned over again. "Black Velvet," she said to her reflection in the glass, remembering the stop she had made at Clarke's on the way home. "What in God's name encouraged me to drink Black Velvet?"

She kept a stack of clean white terry cloth robes on a shelf in the bathroom. She put one on and went into the living room. Ten minutes before five, the clock with the gold face told her. She could get to Dr. Fowler's office almost on time if she hurried and had luck with a cab. But she did not intend to hurry. Sometime during these last hours, tossing and turning in the bed before she fell really asleep, she had decided to get a divorce from Dr. Fowler. What was it the man in the book had called his head shrinker? The foolish psychiatrist, that was it. "I am foolish," he had said, "but not so foolish as the foolish psychiatrist."

Carlotta looked at the clock again. Three hours and fifty-two minutes before she would step out of the wings and walk across the stage to the table with the funny lamp, turn, count, then begin to read the lines that people thought profound.

Doctor Fowler is a fool, she decided, sitting in a deep comfortable chair. He should have discovered by this time that I will not be bullied, even by myself. He should have known better than to offer me his fat and foolish pills.

"Katie!" she called.

"Yes, miss?" Katie's innocent Irish face appeared in the doorway to the kitchen. She was a simple girl and loyal, fond of Carlotta and tolerant.

"Tomato juice, Katie," Carlotta said. "Plenty of Worcestershire sauce. A big glass and cold."

The tomato juice settled her stomach. She felt good. She stretched out her hand at shoulder height, palm down, watching her fingertips with a critical eye. There was no tremor at all. Her nerves were steady. Her head was clear. Even her stomach was all right now, with the heavily seasoned juice inside it. Thank God I quit when I was ahead, she told herself. Thank God I didn't go on with it.

She lit a cigarette and leaned back in the comfortable chair, filled with self-confidence, aware of a heady sense of autonomy, taking keen personal delight in the appearance of her living room. It was spacious and handsome, furnished in the bland modern style. There was a bank of windows and these gave onto a terrace that overlooked the East River. The impact of the room was grey, brain-colored grey, someone had called it, but there were flashes of color, pillows like bright birds, brass at the fire-place, a gilt-framed mirror. There was no color in the pictures that hung on the grey walls. They were all by the same French artist, harsh monochromatic paintings, grey darkening to arid black, with stark, shocking, spidery forms. Carlotta had bought them because they had precise meaning for her, not because the young painter was fashionable. Others disliked them but were impressed because the artist was having a vogue and his prices were high. Over the brick fireplace hung the picture Carlotta liked best: grey and black, spidery, a still life that reproduced a table, a loaf of grey bread, a grey wine glass, a black automatic pistol. Under the painting rested the Oscar she had won for *Breakdown*.

"But darling, how Hollywood can you get?" someone had recently objected. "Oscars on the mantelpiece indeed."

"You are mistaken," Carlotta had said. "It would be really vulgar if I hid it away in a drawer and pretended it did not exist."

She got up now and went to the mantel, picked up the statuette and balanced its weight in her hand, looking at its slick metal surface. It might have been designed to contain very expensive shaving lotion, she thought. Perhaps it should be put away somewhere out of sight. But she did not hide the Oscar away. She put it back in its place on the mantel and went into her bedroom, searching for the bag she had carried last night. She rummaged through it, turning up Doctor Fowler's pills, the eviction notice she had taken from Arthur the Artist, the name and address of the colored singer. In her bag was the letter. She left it there and went to her desk. She wrote a check to Arthur's landlord, put it into an envelope and sealed it, then she wrote a shrewd note to a man whose business it was to arrange things at City Hall. She always carried out promises she had made the night before, no matter how drunk she had been. It was almost a superstition with her, as though in this way she hoped to prevent drink from fulfilling its mission, which was to destroy the truth.

She went into her bedroom and dressed. It was a dark and secret room, heavily curtained, with chocolate-colored walls and a heavy rug, private as a cave. She liked it. No one but she and Katie ever came here. The door was locked when she had guests and they used the other john. I am a Xenophobe, she thought. I fear the stranger as I should fear death.

While she dressed she reflected lazily, going over the things she had done since the moment she left Fowler's office after executing the fish. Clearly she recalled her movements, scrutinized them with a practical eye, and decided she had done nothing that could possibly start a chain reaction of the kind that would oblige her to construct an edifice of lies, excuses, denials and pledges. She had slept with no one, that was certain, insulted no one, encountered no one except for the regulars at Sheridan's, who didn't matter. She was sober now and steady as a rock, ready to walk on stage. There were no consequences. What happened last night might as well have never happened.

"Put it out of your mind, Carlotta," she said to herself as she pulled on her stockings and rubbed them smooth. "Nothing happened. It is all right."

Dressed in a trim brown tweed suit, she returned to the living room, gloves and bag in her hand. Katie Galvin looked at her and said in her gentle brogue, "It's early to go to the theater, miss."

"I have got to eat," Carlotta said.

"I can fix you something here," said Katie. "I can run to the corner and get some chops."

Carlotta touched Katie's cheek. "I am all right," she said firmly. "I know you mean well, Katie, but I promise you that I'm all right."

"Whatever you say, miss," said Katie.

Carlotta left the house. Her mood was good. She was determined to give a demonstration of her will power to Falkstein, to Doctor Fowler, and to herself. I am no alcoholic, she told herself in the elevator, falling as if on a cushion of air, twenty-three stories to the street. Last night, that was nothing. A little relaxation after months of hard work—a few hours respite taken in secret, nothing more, neither the beginning nor the ending of anything.

The air was cool on her cheek. She went for a walk in the romantic evening light, window-shopping on Fifty-seventh Street, looking at gleaming Georgian silver and fragüe Bavarian porcelain. The city was rich and well-groomed in these selected blocks. Carlotta responded to the suave light and the sense of luxuriousness with the conviction that she belonged on these streets in this city. If I am not at home here then I am at home nowhere, she thought.

She went to Sardi's and ate a lamb chop and a salad. All around her people were drinking, show people, press agents; many of them she knew by sight or by name. She was not troubled.

At a table across the room a cowboy star from Hollywood was drinking something or other on the rocks and more of it than was good for him, waving aside the objections of his agent, who sat beside him and fretted because the room was filled with TV people. The actor spotted Carlotta, lifted his glass and winked, then waved: "Come on over!" She smiled and shook her head, feeling powerful self-confidence and a certain sense of superiority. Last night she had been drinking; tonight she was not drinking. It was simple as that, a matter of choice, and be damned to Doctor Fowler and his silent accusative fish.

How did I ever get involved in the psychiatric rat-race? she asked herself, stirring her black sugarless coffee. Head-shrinkers. What was the corny Goldwyn quote? Anyone that goes to a psychiatrist should ought to have his head examined. All that self-pity at thirty dollars the truncated hour. And no absolution. It was a gyp, a swindle, a racket. Once out on the West Coast she had asked a famous and brilliant old actor what he thought of analysis. The old man had answered: "Child, I want my money back."

The cowboy star was waving his arms and attracting attention to himself. People stared. In the silence the voice of the agent could be clearly heard: "It may be nothing but lousy TV but it is also fifteen thousand bucks for fifteen minutes work. That is a thousand dollars a minute. More, if you take time out for the commercials."

"Very good pay," the actor conceded.

"So quit drinking," the agent said.

"I already quit," the cowboy told him.

Carlotta paid her bill and walked uptown to the theater. Little Sabra Sherman was dressed for the lead, fidgeting with her hair, nervous as a child bride.

"Sorry, darling," Carlotta said gaily. "I seem to have recovered. May I have my job back, please?"

Sabra turned quickly as if Carlotta had stuck her with a pin. "Oh, I'm glad," she said.

Carlotta touched the understudy's cheek and asked how it had gone last night.

"Not very well," Sabra told her.

She was a very serious actress, all method and awkwardness. The nose-picking school, Carlotta called it. Turn your back to the audience and scratch your behind. That will make them believe it's real. Poor Sabra must have been hopeless. It was a very demanding part and written to order for one actress, Carlotta McBride, whose method was unique and involved with art.

Ten minutes before curtain Falkstein came to her dressing room, a heavy man with a good cigar, giving off an odor of power mixed with a smell of Havana tobacco and expensive eau de cologne.

"Feeling better?" he said.

"Completely cured," Carlotta answered, not turning around to greet him, facing her make-up mirror. "These mycin drugs are marvelous."

"So are you," Falkstein observed. "Everybody says so, even the *Partisan Review*. But remember one thing, darling. This is the second week in April. The show is sold out solid until November 15, except for the month of August when we close for vacation. If you want to go off the reservation save it until then."

"I am on in thirteen minutes," Carlotta said hostilely. "Will you kindly get out of here so that I can finish dressing?"

Falkstein departed. I detest that man, muttered Carlotta to her reflection. Little hitler. He'd better not try to bully me or I will put him flat on the floor.

She gave a superb performance. There were cheers from the packed house and five curtain calls. It was extraordinary, for a play in its seventh month. Carlotta took the calls, one after the other, bowing humbly to the great public, ashamed because she felt nothing in return for that collective love, out there beyond the footlights, cheering and applauding her.

Riding home in the taxicab she had a sense of triumph unrelated to the quality of her performance, but only to the fact that a performance had been given. She felt like a gambler who has plunged and won. She had shown them, all of them, Falkstein, Fowler, Mickey Sheridan—she had shown them that she was her own master.

Katie helped her undress, then brought hot milk in a mug of the kind children use for cocoa. The mug was one of the few possessions Carlotta had taken from her mother's house. It had been hand-painted to order, then baked in the kiln: CARLOTTA MC BRIDE—Christmas, 1938.

"Leave it, darling," she said to the maid, who put the mug on the night table.

Carlotta went into the bathroom and switched on the light. The oversized medicine cabinet was a small, esoteric pharmacy. There were several dozen bottles from drug stores in Los Angeles and New York—benzedrine, dexadrine, thorazine, codeine, nembutal, seconal, sodium amytal—picker-uppers, calmer-downers, pain-killers, sleeping pills. There were even nitroglycerine capsules of the kind the Hollywood sexual athletes recommended, the capsule crushed with the teeth in common at the moment of climax. Sometime I must try that, she thought idly, running her finger over the bottles. She took two fat capsules from the sodium amytal bottle, swallowed them without water, and went back to her bedroom to drink the hot milk. The room was dark except for her bedside light. She sipped the warm sweet milk and opened the book she was currently reading: Sartre's *Being and Nothingness*. The existentialist convolutions seemed irritating rather than profound. "You belabor the obvious, my friend," she said. Impatiently, she closed the book, let it drop to the floor, and switched off the light. She lay on her back, arms crossed on her bosom, waiting for the pills to work, wondering why she had forgotten to pierce them with a pin. That got the stuff into your system quicker, a Hollywood acquaintance had assured her.

The drug began to work. Carlotta smiled contentedly. The room was dark and warm and safe. Katie was outside. The apartment house was like a fortress, built of steel and stone, guarded by uniformed Irishmen. Her own door was fitted with a chain and a double lock. She was safe in her warm bed in her dark and barricaded room. No stranger could invade. There were men-at-arms in the hall to defend her as she had been defended last night by the plainclothes policemen at Sheridan's. She smiled again in the dark, hugging the warmth, tasting the delicious safety of her guarded bed.

So, protected from harm she slept.

The next day was the bad one. She woke up earlier than she had planned, groggy from the sleeping pills, and sat in the living room, bright with morning light, contriving to make the New York *Times* last until almost ten o'clock.

There were ten empty hours to be filled before it would be time to go to the theater. Why isn't it Thursday or Saturday, matinee day, she asked herself. What a rotten break. A matinee day was exhausting but at least you were busy. The time was filled.

She was nervous and edgy, disinclined to see anyone. She sat in her chair, the exhausted newspaper on the floor beside her, jumpy, aware of the slightest sound. The muscles of her thighs and forearms uttered small involuntary jerks. She was frightened. Yesterday had been easy. She had been giving a demonstration, proving that she could pleasure herself without going into a nose dive, but that had been yesterday. The demonstration had been made. She had performed an act of will...walked the streets, passing bars, gone to Sardi's, then on to the theater and home safe to her own bed. Must she go on demonstrating today and tomorrow and tomorrow and tomorrow?

She went to the bathroom, opened the cabinet, took down the thorazine bottle and shook out two pills, holding them in the palm of her hand. They looked like bright orange buttons. Quickly she swallowed them. They were calmer-downers—clorpromazine—pills that were used in madhouses for patients otherwise kept in strait-jackets or in those odd bathtubs where the water was constantly warm.

She had seen those things, while they were making *Breakdown,* playing the pan of the madwoman whose husband had loved her back to life with the aid of Freud's disciples, warm baths, shock, and occupational therapy. During the last scenes, in the basket-weaving room, she had said, when the cameras were cut: "I would rather be crazy than do this for the rest of my life." And she had ripped to pieces the basket she had pretended to be making.

"My God, I am lonely," she said aloud in her living room. She went to the window, opened it, and stepped out onto the terrace. She was barefoot and the big squares of quarry tile were smooth and cold to the soles of her feet. She leaned on the parapet, staring at the river bright with sun, then at the wasteland of Queens, reaching endlessly to the east, a vast and honeycombed bedroom. She had walked through the streets of Queens; she knew the look of the people who lived there, knew the sound of their voices, knew, almost, their intimate smell. Would I like to be one of them? she asked herself—anonymous, possessed of an anonymous love, safe in my modest comings and goings? Self-pity flooded her veins as if it had been intro-duced to her blood by means of a hypodermic needle. She felt bereft as a Greek martyr, chained to a lonely rock. Who says I don't know my classics? she asked, recalling Sheridan's obser-vation, made the night before. Prometheus. That's classic. How classic can you get? "Ah yes, your grace, but that's in transla-tion." She could hear Mickey's voice, see the long beak of his nose. All at once she yearned to be there, at the bar, on a stool, with Sheridan behind the bar. "No, no, no," she said, arms on the stone guard-rail.

I am lonely, she thought, and shuddered.

How many people do I know in this pesthouse of a city? she asked herself. A hundred? More than that. Two hundred. Three perhaps. Most of them at this hour are at the other end of a telephone line. Hello, darling. Lunch? Dinner? Bonwit-Teller's? Conversation? Copulation? Mutual masturbation? The Museum of Modern Art?

Splendid, splendid, splendid, splendid...

Charming, charming, charming, charming...

Shit, shit, shit, shit....

There were actual men out there in the city who would be happy to pay for her lunch. Normal males with normal voices and the usual physical responses. Of course they know I don't do anything in bed unless I am very drunk indeed, drunk enough so that what happens is a kind of synthetic necrophilia. By this time everyone must know that about me, on this coast and the other coast and way stations in between, including the airless bedrooms on board the Super Chief.

The morning sun warmed her cheek. She leaned over the parapet and looked down at the street. How simple to jump! she thought. That would calm my nerves all right and a damned sight quicker than a basketful of the latest tranquilizer pills.

She stepped back into the living room.

"Katie!" she called. "More coffee. Another pot."

When she was not drinking she lived on coffee—twenty, thirty cups a day, black, sugarless and strong.

"Would you like a sandwich now, miss?" asked Katie when she brought the coffee.

"I'll eat something later," Carlotta said.

"Better to eat," the maid said, as if she uttered an aphorism. "Good to have something on the stomach."

Carlotta sipped the hot fresh coffee, scalding her tongue with the first swallow. She tried to read a novel someone had sent her.

The type page blurred. She put the book aside. She leafed through the fashion magazine, page after page of photographs of girls in the newest dresses, one girl like the other, one dress like the last. In *Vogue* she encountered her own face staring out from the glossy page, a full page photograph. People are talking about...

She read the squib under the heading:

"...the lovely, poetic sense of doom conveyed by Carlotta McBride in the grim but artful *Sunset Gun*, now in its seventh smash month. Here is the beauty of Maud Gonne, who drove mad the poet Yeats, combined with undertones of Concord, Mass. and transcendental-ist purity, plus some mysterious ingredient of acting that is uniquely Carlotta McBride, New York born product of Bryn Mawr College...."

"Wow!" she said out loud.

She remembered the man who had made the photograph for *Vogue,* a mournful, crippled Hungarian clad in black corduroy, kneeling at her feet, lethally intricate camera pointed at her as if it were an implement of prayer, making a great many exposures, moving slowly on his haunches an inch or so at a time, seeking this angle and that. She had been impatient, then apologetic because she disliked being rude except to persons in authority. The exiled Hungarian had shrugged his corduroy shoulders, holding a light meter close to her cheek, and observed politely that one must accept the inconveniences of fame.

The photograph was a good one, honest enough to be disturbing. There was fear in the photographed eyes. The Hungarian must have seen it and sought it out while he clicked away, making a hundred odd negatives. Will others see it? Carlotta wondered, closing the magazine, letting it slide from her lap to the floor.

She looked around the big room. What caught her eye was her pocketbook, on the desk where she had left it after writing the check and the letter. She went to the desk and opened the bag, taking out the letter from the detective agency. For the twentieth time she read it:

MULLIGAN AND MULLIGAN
(formerly agents Federal Bureau of Investigation)
1740 Broadway
New York City
INVESTIGATIONS DISCREETLY UNDERTAKEN

SUBJECT: Michael McBride

Dear Miss McBride:

Our French associates have located above subject in Paris, France. Last known address, 48 bis rue de Tournon, Paris.

Do you wish us to pursue the matter further? We await your instructions.

Sincerely,
Vincent Mulligan
Vice President

She folded the letter and put it back into her purse. For three days now she had carried it about, afraid to mention it to Doctor Fowler, afraid to accept the intelligence it contained, afraid to go at once to Paris, afraid to tear the letter to bits and leave things as they had been.

She crossed the room quickly and recrossed, tiger in cage, prisoner pacing his cell. The sense of confinement was maddening. *I must get out of here,* she said. *I must get out of here.*

A movie. That was the answer.

One could always hide in a movie.

It is dark, one is alone, and they don't serve drinks.

She took a bath and dressed and told Katie to expect her for supper.

"Will you be going to the doctor then, miss?"

"No more," said Carlotta firmly. "I am finished with him. One hundred percent cured. I think he's going to ask me for a testimonial letter."

She put the bottle of thorazine pills into her bag and walked across town. At one of the snobbish art theaters she paused and looked at the posters. The film was a new one and in French. I am perverse, she thought, as she bought a ticket and went down the ramp into the plush dark, to seat herself in a comfortable chair.

The scene was Paris, the season spring, the subject illicit love. It was a very handsome film, filled with grey Parisian tristesse, love scenes played with literalness, down to the lacerated underpants dropped upon the figured rug, caught by the camera's eye and held for a second, two seconds. Carlotta sat in the deep chair, watching the screen and eating thorazine pills as if they were peanuts. The label said: Two each, three times daily, for nerves.

Carlotta knew better than that.

At the madhouse in the desert where they made *Breakdown,* they fed these pills by the cupful to the schizos and paranoids that populated the place, or so she had been told. Side effects? Very rare, Miss McBride. We have a case or two of jaundice, but very rare. Very rare. Of course if the liver is diseased, that is another matter.

My liver is all right, Carlotta thought contentedly, swallowing the pills. What is it the old drunks get? Hobnailed liver, that's it. Wonderful. Graphic phrase.

Watching the young love in Paris she became sentimental, then depressed. She looked at Paris on the big screen. The camera was in a taxicab, crossing the river to the Place de la Concorde. The photography was evocative and very beautiful. Then there were soft words in French, a long mucilaginous kiss and a long Gallic sigh. Carlotta was struck by a wave of blind elemental jealousy and a sharp awareness of rejection unfocused but powerful.

She began to weep softly. There was a man beside her, white face blurred in the dark. "Is anything wrong, miss?" he asked.

She crowded past his knees and hurried up the carpeted ramp, blind flight, tears in her eyes. There was a lounge with a coffee urn and an offering of blue-green cups and saucers. It was empty. Carlotta stopped and fixed her face, using the dark blue mirror that covered one of the walls. She helped herself to coffee and drank it standing up. It was tepid and bitter; she drank three cups, then went out into the street.

Shall I call Doctor Fowler?

Call me if you are in trouble, he had said.

She stood in front of the theater, the taste of the coffee in her mouth, her knees trembling under her skirt so that her thighs came together in a flabby rhythm, flesh against flesh, uncontrollable as shivering. She was on the edge of hysteria and she understood this with clinical precision. Silently, Doctor Fowler's fish swam before her closed eyes. Her body trembled. She swallowed, forcing the trembling to stop, then opened her eyes. She sighed for herself and then moved quickly toward the doom she wanted, passing through the doors of a cheap saloon on Broadway, a few steps from the movie house.

"A dry martini, please," she said, her voice in a low, conspiratorial register.

That is the quickest thing, she thought, a four to one martini, the unequivocal drink. She watched the barman stir the mixture of gin, vermouth and ice and watched him pour skillfully so that the glass was precisely filled, nothing left in the mixer but ice. He took a segment of lemon peel and snapped it over the glass, a conclusive pantomime, like wringing the neck of a chicken. Carlotta wet her lips. The drink was in front of her on the bar. Behind her was a country of terror. She had the irrational but positive conviction that she was pursued by those empowered to punish her. She waited for a significant footstep, an authorized hand on her shoulder, steel handcuff on her wrist. There was nothing, no sound, no breath on the back of her neck. Listlessly the bartender polished glasses with a clean towel. Carlotta leaned forward, took the martini in both hands, touched it with her lips, emptied it. The effect was like that of a blow in the pit of the stomach. She shuddered, holding her lips tightly together, refusing to vomit. After a little her stomach surrendered to her will. The drink stayed down. The alcohol warmed her blood.

She drank three martinis, then went out into the street. The need to scream was gone. She walked through the shabby afternoon crowd along the honky-tonk street. YOUR PHOTO WHILE YOU WAIT. COTTON CANDY. SOUVENIRS. PAPAYA JUICE. 10,000 PINUPS—*we specialize.* Lonely, innocent-eyed sailors walked in pairs, undirected, turning away from the Levantine pimps who lounged against the drugstore windows, wearing cheap new clothes and obscenely narrow shoes. Guiltless and gaping strangers mixed in the crowd with the scum of the city. Near the statue of Father Duffy an old actor sunned himself and fed bread crumbs from a bag to the pigeons.

Carlotta had a malicious, rejected impulse to drink a dozen martinis, then go to the doctor's office and present herself for inspection. He had never seen her drunk. Contemptuously she wondered had he ever seen anyone drunk, outside of a hospital ward. She had no use for A.A. but the smug bastards had one thing right: only a lush can understand a lush. Everyone else is on the outside looking in. That had been the trouble with her husband, the good Doctor Eric. Poor Eric, she said to herself, out in the sexual cold, outside the advertised body of his own wedded wife. Yet how much worse when she had drugged herself with whiskey and pretended. It must have been like making love to a department store mannikin. For her it had been loathsome as a doctor's examination on the table with stirrups, a gross invasion of privacy, distasteful as an enema.

She walked east through a tawdry street, past secretive cheap hotels that invited: Transients-Permanent. I am both, she said to herself. I am the permanent transient. She stopped at a bar and drank a martini, then continued to walk uptown, stopping whenever she wanted a drink, walking, she thought, without direction, until with a sense of shock she found herself on the corner of Madison Avenue and Sixty-seventh Street. Why am I here? she asked herself. Have I returned to the scene of the crime? Against her will but drawn by an impulse like the one that obliges us to look on the dead against our desires, she moved through the familiar street, stopping when she came to the house, looking up at the windows of the room that had once been hers. I know where he is, she said to herself. You don't know, but I know. I know the name of the city, the name of the street.

At the window of the front room den, she saw her mother's silhouette. She stood at the curb, frozen, stabbed by need, unable to enter the house and rejoin the necessary battle. She walked, then began to run, until she reached the corner and the safety of a taxicab. She sat in the cab, trembling. I will not go to Sheridan's. I will not. I will not. She gave the address of a smart bar in the east Fifties near Park Avenue.

It was a dark expensive bar with white plaster cupids in niches, heavy curtains, a rug that had been woven to order so that the name of the place was endlessly repeated in a monogram that looked like a bug. A man and woman sat in conference beyond the curve of the bar, heads together, speaking inaudibly, drinks neglected. Are they plotting murder or just divorce? Carlotta asked herself. Or simply trying to reach agreement on where to have dinner or which play to see? They were the only customers. The place was depressingly silent, the atmosphere almost illicit.

"Doesn't anyone drink anymore?" Carlotta said to the bartender when he served her martini.

"You never know," he told her. "Sometimes, three o'clock this place is jammed. Other times it's like this. People are funny, the way they drink."

"You can say that again," Carlotta agreed.

At the sound of voices, the conspiratorial pair looked up. They recognized Carlotta and for some minutes stared at her, trying not to be offensive. At last the woman said shyly, in a mid-western accent, "Excuse our staring, Miss McBride, but we saw you in *Breakdown*. We thought you were great."

"Thank you," Carlotta said.

"How does it feel, I mean, playing a part like that?" the woman asked. "Pretending to be a crazy person, I mean."

"Mentally ill, Julia," her companion said reproachfully. "Not crazy. Mentally ill."

Carlotta considered the woman's question. Doctor Fowler once had asked her almost the same question. She had laughed and wanted to know if paranoia was contagious. Sometimes, he had told her gravely, refusing as always to be amused. Now she smiled at the woman and said, "An actress is just a machine, you know. A voice, a face, a body, controlled by the lines in a script and the instructions of a director. Mad woman, Queen of England, adolescent from Verona, lost little rich girl. They're all just parts. What difference does it make?"

"Oh," said the woman. "Oh, I see." She hesitated, then said, "We are going to see you tonight, Miss McBride. We got tickets for your show from one of those scalpers. Cost us a fortune."

"I hope you will think it was worth the money," Carlotta said, asking for another drink.

When the mid-western couple had gone she raised her head and in the darkened mirror saw the familiar eye of her reflection. She had not given a truthful answer. *Breakdown* had left scars on her soul. It is possible to injure even a machine and she had been injured. Sometimes it was difficult to believe that she had not actually been mad for a time and locked away behind green lawns and carefully barbered shrubbery, laced into a canvas jacket, locked on a table and subjected to partial electrical execution, washed in the warm Blood of the Lamb, flowing through the therapeutic tubs. "Another picture like this one, I'll be nutty as a fruitcake myself," one of the camera crew had said. Everyone had felt it during the weeks they lived at the hospital but no one had felt it as much as Carlotta.

The despair dredged up by the French film was now dissolved in gin; the sense of being pursued was gone. Carlotta was in a state of suspension, almost at her ease. Stage two, she told herself. Stage one was the fear and terror, the near puking at the first drink, the sudden blow between the eyes as the alcohol took effect. Then one leveled off into this false euphoria.

How odd that it always worked!

"One thing about alcohol, it works," Doctor Fowler had told her. "It may destroy a man's career, ruin his marriage, turn him into a zombie unconscious in a hallway—but it works. On short term it works much faster than a psychiatrist or a priest or the love of a husband or a wife. Those things, love, therapy, faith in God, they all take time. They must be developed, constructed, if you like. And they aren't always available. Wives sometimes are false. The doctor may be on vacation. Sometimes God refuses to be believed in. But alcohol is always there ready to go to work at once. Ten minutes, half an hour, the little formless fears are gone or turned into harmless amusement." "But they come back," she had observed. "Oh yes, and they bring reinforcements," he had agreed.

The little formless fears. They lurked in the tropical shrubbery in scenes in *The Emperor Jones*. What were they like for O'Neill himself, sitting at a lopsided table in the place he called Jimmy the Priest's? She had played in a college production of *Beyond the Horizon*. It was that performance that brought her to Stockbridge and from Stockbridge to Broadway. Afterward she had studied O'Neill as if the plays were a kind of scripture. Unholy Writ. Mad doomed Irish wit, mixed with anguish, bathed in complicated genius.

Two Irishmen, two Irishmen, were digging in a ditch
One called the other one a dirty son-of-a-....

She hummed idly, tapping the bar. I am becoming drunk, she thought, matter-of-factly, without fear. You are drunk, but you are not Irish, fiercely she insisted to herself. It is not always the same thing. You are the permanent transient, left on a doorstep in Antwerp, blistered in Brussels, patched and peeled in London, inhabitant of a rented house, where the Jew squats under the sill. "Merds, rat, broken glass." She tried to quote and the lines escaped her. You are too old for Eliot or he is too old for you, she said.

You are the native of no state and you shall not inherit the earth, she said to herself without pity.

Once she had talked with a professor at the New York School of Social Work, in a big room in an old mansion built by Andrew Carnegie. He had written a book about foundlings and someone had given her a letter to him.

"Nineteen twenty-nine or thirty?" the professor had said. "You must remember, my dear child, that was in the great depression. People were sleeping in the parks. There were soup kitchens and so on. Your natural parents may simply have found themselves unable to feed you. Quite possibly they were respectable people who loved you and thought they were doing the right thing. As for attempting to trace them..." the professor had shrugged his shoulders. "It would be one chance in a million. The birth may not have been registered, if no doctor attended your mother. I'm afraid you will find it a cold trail."

There's a cold, cold trail awinding....

After her visit to the professor, she had gone to the public library and looked at newspaper photographs of the Hoovervilles and Shantytowns and Prosperity Villages, where certain people had had their existence at about the time she was born. Sometimes she pictured the scene for herself: the cabin made of orange crates, under a rusting tin roof, the mother accouched on a dirt floor, neighbor women attending her pain, bathing the child and the woman's thighs with water boiled in a lard can over an urban campfire. Did she have milk, my mother, I wonder? Did she feed me once, before she wrapped me in half a blanket and carried me to the railroad station or the church door? Where did she leave me, I wonder, and what did she feel as she turned away?

She sat drinking the chilled gin, brooding over her parentage, exhuming old phantasies, legends of foundlings and changelings and long lost princesses of the blood. Anastasia had aphasia. The Royal Family of Hooverville, hard by the New York Central tracks. What are you complaining about? she demanded impatiently of herself. Jesus was born in a manger and his bed was made of hay. But he will have a second coming. How can I have a second coming if I never had a first?

Stop it! she said sharply to herself.

The bar now was filled with people. She looked at her watch. Five-thirty. It was incredible. It must be later. She had the conviction that she had been sitting here for days. It seemed that time declined to pass. But the alcoholic clock is unreliable. People were crowding around her, laughing and drinking. She was laughing and drinking with them. Suddenly it was eight o'clock and she was frightened. She paid her bill and went into the street: "Taxi! Taxicab!"

She uttered the name of the theater and sat back in the seat, her arms heavy. At the stage door she was staggering. The stage doorman helped her out of the cab and guided her to her dressing room. She sat down in front of the mirror and switched on the battery of lights. She unbuttoned the top of her dress and slipped out of it, sitting down. She reached for cold cream and Kleenex and began to make up very carefully, her eyes fixed in dead focus on the nose of her image in the mirror. The lights seemed to move toward her. There was a fog of gin that smothered her, as if her face was covered by an anesthetist's mask. She leaned forward with a sense of going under and rested her head on the dressing table. She could not fight back.

For a few seconds she emerged from the fog. She was in a taxicab. There were a man and a woman. The swaying cab made her ill. She woke up next at four in the morning, terrified and lost. There were ashes in her mouth and her eyeballs ached. She touched her eyes with her fingers, pressing hard. There were rockets and shooting stars and geometric figures of neon green, fading reluctantly into the dark. She felt the sheets. They were smooth-textured, expensive. This cannot be Bellevue, then. "Katie!" she cried out. "Katie, I want you!"

Katie appeared in the bedroom doorway, wearing a white flannel robe, black Irish hair on her shoulders. There was a light behind her. Carlotta sat up in bed. "I am thirsty," she said. Katie brought her a glass of water and smoothed the sheets. "Go to sleep now, miss," she said. "The doctor gave you a shot of something he said would make you sleep. Don't try to be fighting it."

Carlotta felt of her buttocks, right, then left. There was a sore place where the needle had entered her flesh. "What doctor?" she demanded. "What was his name?"

"Some doctor I never seen before," Katie said. "Mr. Falkstein called him after he brought you home."

Falkstein, Carlotta thought. God damn his soul to hell.

"All right then, Katie," she said. "Leave a light in the living room, will you?"

When Katie had gone back to bed, Carlotta got up and went to the bathroom. Her bladder was full and aching. She sat limply on the pot, trying to urinate, but she could not pass water. She gave it up and took two nembutal capsules from the medicine chest. With a pin she punched holes in them, then swallowed them down, tasting the faint bitterness that seeped through the pinholes. She got back into bed, trying to remember. She could not force her mind to retrace her movements beyond the plush little bar and the cold martinis. She did not remember the theater. But how did Falkstein get into it then? Did they send for him, at the bar? Were there police? The nembutal rescued her from the hopeless pursuit of her lost hours. She fell into a deep sleep, breathing heavily through her mouth. From time to time Katie looked in at her through the door.

Late in the afternoon she woke up, with difficulty and to pain. There was a double hangover from the various drugs and the alcohol. For a long time after she became conscious she was unable to get up. She tried to raise her head from the pillow and was immediately struck by vertigo and nausea. After perhaps an hour she succeeded in sitting on the edge of the bed. The darkened room turned dangerously. *Don't move!* she commanded herself. The complex of experience came into play. She knew that if she did not move, sooner or later the dizziness would pass or retreat enough so that she could stand. When that happened she lurched to the bathroom and sloshed her face with cold water. She sat on the toilet seat. "Relax," she said to herself. "Relax." The urine spurted from her body. The sensation of relief was exquisite. She remained on the toilet, waiting. Soon the nausea would subside. Then she could have a drink and possibly hold it down. She was nude. In the mirror bolted to the bathroom door she saw the reflection of her body. There were bruises on her thighs, black and blue, sore to the touch. She had bumped into things last night, furniture, the door of a cab, a fire hydrant on the street, but she had felt nothing then. It is a precise expression: *feeling no pain.* She pinched the muscles of her thighs and arms, trying to shock herself out of the sick numbness, to feel pain, bright and sharp, signalling that she was alive, that the blood flowed in her veins. She got up from the toilet seat, put on a clean terry cloth robe and went barefoot to the living room.

In a chair sat Falkstein, reading the manuscript of a play, hat, coat and briefcase on the floor beside him.

"Make yourself at home," Carlotta said. "We always welcome the overflow from the public library."

Falkstein put the manuscript into his briefcase. "Never mind that," he said. "Your maid let me in. Now you try to get some black coffee into your stomach. I want to talk to you."

"I don't feel like talking," she said. "If you want conversation go downtown to the Players Club."

"Shut up and sit down," said Falkstein.

He went to the kitchen and spoke to Katie. In a few minutes Carlotta sat with a cup and saucer on her lap. The coffee was fresh and very hot. She scalded her mouth again, but the warmth in her stomach was reassuring.

"As far as I'm concerned you can go straight to the gutter," Falkstein told her, and there was no doubt that he meant it.

"The last time I talked to my accountant he told me I had about two hundred thousand dollars and very shrewdly invested," Carlotta said. "Why should I sleep in the gutter when there's a good bed here?"

"So by-pass the gutter for a couple of years," Falkstein said. "You'll get to it sooner or later, if you don't hit the booby hatch first."

Carlotta spilled coffee on her leg. "Jesus!" she exclaimed. "That's hot."

"You are getting a break," Falkstein said, ignoring her sharp momentary pain. "Not for your own sake. You don't deserve it. But a play is a joint enterprise. There are other people involved, and they do deserve a break."

"Let Sabra take over," Carlotta said wearily. "I am tired. Tired and bored."

"Sabra can't do it," said Falkstein. "The part was written for you, Carlotta. Nobody else can do it."

"I am sick of the god damned play," Carlotta said fiercely. "Close it and the hell with it."

"This is Wednesday. We are closing until next Monday," Falkstein told her. "We sent a note to the papers this morning, announcing that you were sick."

"That is no press agent's lie," Carlotta said.

Falkstein poked a finger at her; the clear polish of his manicure glittered like a malevolent eye. "You are getting a break, McBride," he said. "We reopen Monday night. If you are not on stage, clean sober and ready to work, I will cut your throat from ear to ear. I will crucify you, do you hear me? I will bring charges with Equity. I will sue you for every nickel you've got. I will spread the whole dirty story through the gossip magazines and the gutter press. I have been around for a long time and I know all the angles. When I get through with you, young lady, you won't be able to get a part in West Pessary, Nebraska."

He stood up and buttoned his double-breasted coat, strode to the windows, looked at the sky with disfavor, and turned back to Carlotta. He is like a policeman, she thought. The precinct lieutenant, honest and tough, in a grade-B story of cops and robbers.

"Talent? Sure you've got talent," he said, coat reopened, thumbs in his vest. "So did Jack Barrymore. He had more than talent, maybe, but it didn't save him. And you're a three-time loser already, baby. You were in trouble in Hollywood. You were in trouble with me last year. Now you're in trouble with me again." He counted on his glittering fingers: one, two, three. "Three strikes and out," he said. "Only this time we're going to call it a foul tip, if you straighten out by Monday night."

"You sound like God," said Carlotta. "Didn't anyone tell you I don't believe in God anymore?"

"I sound like a man who is responsible to an author, a cast of people, and a group of investors. And maybe to the public. I wouldn't know. I don't know what you believe in. I don't give a god damn. But I'll tell you this, sweetheart. If you don't believe in your own talent then you don't believe in anything and you might as well be dead."

"Then please go away and let me die," Carlotta said amiably. "It is a thing I prefer to do when there are no strangers about."

"Keep out of sight, do you hear?" Falkstein said bluntly. "Go to Towns or to Knickerbocker or better still to that joint in Connecticut. Sweat the booze out of your system and try to behave like a grown-up girl."

He picked up his hat and his briefcase and departed without saying goodbye. As soon as the door closed behind him Carlotta went to the liquor cabinet and poured a drink of whiskey—a big one, three or four ounces, poured into a tumbler so that it would not spill when her hand shook. She held the glass in her hand, looking at it as though the liquid it held were alive. She began to shake violently as a malaria patient. She gulped down the liquor. After a moment she poured another drink, waited a moment, and drank it. She retched and shuddered, lost her breath, caught the back of a chair for support. It was a punishing cure but it was the only cure she knew this side of a padded cell.

She went back to her chair and sat down, waiting for the whiskey to work. She had faith in the whiskey, more than she had in anything else. It had never failed her.

It did not fail her now.

In an hour the intimations of death were gone. She felt, if not positively good, at least able to face the day. She sat huddled in her chair and reflected upon her situation. Falkstein's professional brutality had not frightened her. In Hollywood she had learned not to be frightened of producers who made threats. "When they make threats they are scared and they need you," someone had advised her. "When they're finished with you they ignore you." As for the five days' vacation, she was entitled to it, after half a year of work, carrying this bloody play on her back, working like a Chinese coolie. "Keep out of sight," Falkstein had said. "Go to the Hartford Retreat or Towns or Knickerbocker."

She had no intention of going to any of these places. She wanted to go to Paris, and nowhere else. It wasn't easy. There would be passports and passenger lists and a corporal's guard of reporters. They would hound her, with their photographers, from the moment she got to the airport at Idlewild.

She brooded over the problem, taking a drink from time to time, self-consciously making them small ones. Katie came into the living room, bearing a tray with fresh coffee. As she went back to the kitchen, Carlotta was struck by an idea. She and Katie were almost the same size. Katie wore her discarded clothes without alteration. Katie was a year or two younger, but that didn't matter. Hair was the only problem. Carlotta's hair was a fine silky blonde, almost ash. Katie's was dark, with an undertone of blue-black, the color of ink. Hair, thought Carlotta. Hair is nothing.

"Katie!" she called.

"Yes, miss?"

"Do you have the passport you used last year when you went home to see your people?"

"Yes, miss," said Katie. Carlotta had financed the trip home, paid the air fare and Katie's wages.

"Would you loan it to me?" Carlotta asked.

Katie had a rebel streak in her that enjoyed any kind of conspiracy. Authority was her natural enemy. She got her passport from a drawer and handed it to Carlotta. REPUBLIC OF IRELAND, Carlotta read, and then the Gaelic: *Poblacht nã h Eireann* and then the French: Republique d'Irlande. It was a small green book, stamped on the cover with a golden harp. She stood up, filled with excitement. "What a mad idea!" she thought. "What a brilliantly mad idea!"

She called Air France. "Non-stop to Paris," she said. "Yes please, a berth. Name? Kathleen Galvin. Irish passport."

It will be simple, simple, simple, she said to herself. At Orly they hardly look at your passport, as long as you are respectably dressed.

She went to the bank and cashed a check, then went to the place in Radio City and bought an enormous quantity of francs, getting the grey market price.

"Pounds, miss?" the clerk said. "West German marks?"

"Nothing but francs," Carlotta said, tucking the money into her purse.

She went to a beauty parlor on Lexington Avenue and asked them to dye her hair blue-black. "Ah miss, it's a crime," the girl protested. "It's just for a part in a play," said Carlotta. She was filled with purpose now. This is what I've been wanting to do all along, she said to herself. She had been timing her drinks through the day—one an hour, no more no less—and her mind was clear. It was a drunkard's crafty trick she had learned from an old Irish character man who once had played her father in a picture. "Keeps you alive, my dear," he had said. "And you never get out of control. Of course by sundown you're tiddly but by then it doesn't matter."

By sundown I shall be drinking champagne and talking in French with the stewardess, Carlotta assured herself. Behind her the motor of the dryer hummed and warm air caressed her scalp. When her hair was dry she inspected herself in the beauty shop mirror. The effect was extraordinary. She decided she rather liked it.

She went home to pack her bags, paying no attention to the stares of the doormen and elevator boys.

"If anyone calls, tell them I've gone to Arden's place in Arizona for a rest," she said to Katie. "Tell them I'm using a fake name and that you don't know what it is. I'll be back on Monday, maybe before that."

Katie could read the signs and she knew that the time for persuasion was past. It would do no good to bully her mistress or to attempt to cajole her. The barometer was falling; God Almighty Himself could not now call off the storm.

Carlotta was exhilarated, heading toward the eye of the storm. She called a Carey Cadillac to take her to Idlewild. Driving through the wastes of Queens she debated with Doctor Fowler. "You don't approve of my journey?" she said. "Well, you are wrong. I am on my way to Paris, France, to bring back a soldier who never came home. It is unfinished business, Doctor Fowler. A matter that must be cleared up, and not in your office, my friend." She closed her eyes and sat back on the cushions, lulled by the elegant movement of the car. "Fowler, you couldn't help me," she said. "I talked and you listened to me and I paid you and I came every day but you did not help me. All that costly conversation. It did no good at all. It is not fair, it is not fair ...."

CHAPTER FOUR

MOURNING, THEY SAY, BECOMES ELECTRA

Months ago she had tried to tell Doctor Fowler why she must find him and bring him back or at least touch his hand, ask him to forgive her or have him beg to be forgiven.

—Last night I tried to sleep with a man, she had said. It was before she had moved to the chair beside the doctor's desk. She was on the couch. Doctor Fowler was behind her; she could not see him.

—He is a nice young man, she went on. A writer. My age, perhaps, or a few years older. He is tall and straight and he has strong and beautiful hands. And he is intelligent. We met at a cocktail party. It was yesterday. Sunday. I was drinking ginger ale and eating too many lukewarm miniature sausages. He was drinking cloudy martinis, poured from a pitcher by the host. We talked. About my play and then about a certain group of French novelists in whom we seemed to have a mutual interest. "Will you have dinner with me?" he said, when it was time to leave the party. "Come home and I'll cook your dinner," I said. "I know there's a steak in my ice box. I liked him, you see, and I thought perhaps that being a writer he really couldn't afford to be buying dinners for people like me. There was nothing romantic, you understand. We were simply sophisticated grown up people attracted one to the other.

She broke off, fixing her eyes on a point in the ceiling. Then she began to cry.

—I am crying, she said. You can't see, but I am crying.

Doctor Fowler handed her a Kleenex taken from the box he kept in a drawer of his desk.

—Damn you, she said. Damn you.

He waited in the chair behind her. He always waited, impassive as an idol, while the silent electric clock swept away the time.

—It was the first time in years I have tried to sleep with a man without having made myself drunk first, she said. I thought it was going to work. Right up until the moment he got into the bed beside me I thought it was going to work. He had kissed me in the other room and it had been all right. He had even touched my breast or at least the cloth that covered my breast. "I have changed," I said to myself. "Doctor Fowler has somehow helped me to change." I was mistaken. I put perfume behind my ears and perfume in the gorge of my breasts. I got into my soft bed and watched him while he took off his clothes. "Leave the light on," he said. "No," I said. "No." I switched it off. In the dark he moved toward me. He got into the bed with me, young and hard and throbbing with life. I touched him. It was as though I had touched a high tension wire. My body stiffened. I was rigid. I could feel the chill enter my blood, as if iced water were being fed into my veins. He tried to kiss me. I was ill, actively, vomitously ill on the clean sheets of my own bed. "I'm sorry," he said. "Another time, maybe." He dressed in the dark and went away. I lay in the bed beside the vomit. He was there with me, Michael McBride, there in the dark room with me, except that it was my bedroom no longer. It was the bedroom at the Lodge, bright with winter sun, and he stood in the little john, naked, powerful as a bull, the scar of the bullet on his leg, holding himself and pissing away in a steady stream that would not stop. "Stop it!" I shouted in the dark. "Stop it, stop it, stop it!" He was there like a permanent statue. I leaped out of bed and turned on the light. I went into the next room and poured a drink of whiskey. "This will make it go away," I said to myself. "If I had taken a quart of this, that young man and I would be making love at this moment, staining the bed with our copulations instead of with my vomit." I did not drink the whiskey. I poured it back into the bottle, changed the sheets on my bed, took a pill and tried to sleep.

—You should have called me, Doctor Fowler said. I told you to call me if you were in trouble.

—It is not you I want, Carlotta said. It is not you, my dear Fowler. It is Michael McBride.

—You can find him here in this room, as much of him as you need, the Doctor said.

—That is nonsense, Carlotta said.

She lay on the couch for a long time, Doctor Fowler behind her, waiting, waiting for her to talk. At last she spoke again:

There was a letter from Arizona, she said. I saw it on the silver tray in the morning, mixed with innocuous mail. His handwriting is square and simple, written always in black ink with a square-tipped pen. I recognized it at once. I almost opened the letter though it was not addressed to me. I held it in my hands, turning it over. There was no return address.

It was late and I should have started for school but I waited in the dining room until mother came down. She read the letter, read it again, then tore it across and across again.

"When is he coming home?" I asked.

"He is not coming home," she answered.

"But he lives here," I said. "How can he not come home?"

"He is not coming," she said firmly. "He is never coming."

She was dressed in a black cashmere sweater, long sleeved, with a high neck. There were pearls at her throat. With her black hair drawn back she looked formal as a nun.

"Where is he?" I demanded. "I have a right to know where he is."

She picked up the pieces of letter. "When he wrote this he was in Tucson," she said. "He is not there now. He does not say where he plans to go, only that he will not come here."

I did not go to school that day. I went up the stairs to my bedroom and cried. In the afternoon I went out for a walk. It was January but the day was warm. I walked east toward the river. There was a bench in the sunlight and from the bench I could see the water. I sat there for several hours, smoking cigarettes. I must have known that he was not ever going to come back to me or to her or to that house, but it was an idea my mind had declined to accept. "I can't go on living with her after what has happened," I had said to him in the car when we returned from the Lodge. "You must, Carlotta," he had said. "You must."

I looked at the river, at a point where the water swirled around an outcropping of rock. Then I shivered. The sun was gone and it was cold. I got up and walked back to the house. In the kitchen I made a sandwich and poured a glass of milk, eating and drinking standing up at the cook's work counter. Then I telephoned one of the girls and told her that I had been ill with the flu. She gave me the day's assignments and I went up to my room and sat down to my work. His photograph was on my desk. He was smiling, the happy soldier, responsible to nothing but death. I put the picture away in the bottom drawer of my desk and got on with my homework.

My instinct was to run away, to change my name, to disappear and wander the earth until I found that I had stopped somewhere, at some signal, and in that place to create an identity to replace the one I had lost. Surely, I thought, somewhere out in the world there must be an identity that had been created for me. I did not go. There has always been a practical germ in my temperament, a hard little center of ego that makes me look after myself, steers me just this side or that of the pits and potholes that attract me and thus enables me to avoid destruction. I was too young for the world and I knew it. I had no education, no experience of life, no skill that would make my living. If I departed, thief in the night, I would not even have the money to which I was entitled for impersonating Carlotta McBride. I stayed on in my mother's house like a crab hiding under a rock, waiting for his shell to develop and harden. I had my two dark secrets and they remained in my heart, ticking away like twin time-bombs, but not heard by anyone else.

Half of the girls at my school went to the College of Mount St. Vincent. I was supposed to go with them. It was where my mother had been when she was married. In the spring of my last year I told her I would not go. "What will you do, then?" she asked. "If you give me the money I shall go to Bryn Mawr," I told her. "If not I will get a job and go to Hunter College." "Bryn Mawr?" she said. "But that is a Protestant college, Carlotta." "It is non-sectarian," I told her. "So am I."

She gave me the money.

It was an English professor at college who suggested that I try out for the female lead in a production of *Beyond the Horizon* that was being put on in Philadelphia by a group of students from three colleges on the Main Line. "But I'm not an actress," I told him. He was sagacious and very worldly, a white-haired man who wrote minor novels. "Oh, yes," he said. "You are a born actress."

I read the play, then I read for the part. I got it. Even in rehearsal I understood that the professor had been right. I was an actress, a born actress.

They say there are two kinds of actresses—the intuitive kind, who feels the part, and the cerebral kind, who studies it out. I think perhaps that I am both. The first night in Philadelphia when I walked out onto the stage I knew that I had found a metier, whatever else I had failed to find on that pretty campus. I was an actress and a good one. I would be rich and famous, independent, the queen of my own world.

I am an actress. In the theater, even in Hollywood, I feel innocent when I am playing a part, and the innocence lasts until the part wears out.

Don't misunderstand me, Doctor. I did not burst on the waiting world fully made. I worked hard every summer, at Stockbridge, in Massachusetts. I worked hard in college plays. And I read, I studied, I analyzed, I steeped myself in the art and the lore of the theater. It seemed to me that the theater might be the answer to my problem. There on the stage were identities for me, by the dozens, by the thousands. To assume them, all one wanted was talent, energy and the will to work.

And luck. One must not forget luck.

Six months after I finished college I had a part on Broadway. It was a revival of *Anna Christie* and I was a sensation. I am a good actress. Not as good as they say I am, but good. The day after we opened I read the reviews in the morning papers. I was at home, in the dining room. I read the *Times,* then the *Herald Tribune,* then I went upstairs to my bedroom and began to pack my clothes.

I moved into a corner room in the Plaza Hotel and stepped out into the world, taking my secrets with me but hidden away where they could not be seen by other people.

I think that I was never unaware of the question mark that had been made a permanent part of my being, but people did not know. I did not let them know.

At college I was Carlotta McBride, a handsome girl with a flair for clothes, always near the top of the class, interested in literature and dramatics. At Stockbridge I was Carlotta McBride, a hard-working girl with talent. Sometimes it amused me. I felt like a light-colored Negro who passes for white, fooling them all, even his own people. I kept my assumed identity and my assumed name, or rather the name and identity that had been assumed for me when I was swaddled and helpless.

In Hollywood the studio wanted to change my name. I refused. It was my own alias and I was determined to keep it until I found a name of my own or a false name that suited me better. I thought it was a splendid joke, out there on the Coast. Everyone had a made-up name except for me. I was the pigheaded mick who refused to take what the studio offered, out of some stubborn Hibernian pride.

I was never afraid of the studio in the way most people out there are afraid. When I went to the Coast for my first picture I took it for granted that I would be a success and of course I was a success. When I started as an actress, I felt in my heart as though I had been a professional all my life. "How long have you been acting, child?" someone asked me, on the set of my first picture. "I have been acting all my life," I said complacently. And it was true. I was an actress. I am an actress. I cannot imagine myself being anything else but an actress. If I were drunk in the gutter or flat on my back in a whore house or locked up in a madhouse, I would be playing a part, the part of Carlotta McBride. If I were to stop playing my part I would instantly be nothing, a tin can without a label, a blank application form, a book printed in a language that no one on earth can read, or one of those books not printed at all, consisting of blank pages bound up so that the publisher will know how much the book will weigh. If I did not act I would be nothing and so I go on acting, drunk, sober, working, resting, I go on acting.

Search for identity, I said, when we started to talk about the disappearance of my ancestry. It is a search I have been making. Everyone looks first in books, if he has been exposed to books in schools and other places.

All aluvial, arm alluvial. Spread your washing proper. Drink deep of the Liffey water. That is Joyce, Doctor. Or almost Joyce.

I have been through the Earwicker search, with the aid of a key and a college professor. It is a blind Dublin alley with nothing at the end but another question, or is it another gargantuan yawn? In the end is the beginning. In my end is my beginning. Blind alleys by blind authors, appropriately exiled and Irish. Literature is a trap with dull jaws. Give me a ballad-singer anytime. I can cry over Irish slop as I never rejoiced over Joyce. Stop using that fake brogue. This is a Protestant doctor's office, not a public house in Ballykelly.

I know. You are asking yourself what it is that I am trying to avoid by berating Mr. Joyce, which sure to heaven is an old game now. All in good time, my boyo. It is my money on the bar, not yours. You be quiet and pour the whiskey and mop the bar when it wants mopping. Why is it that you never ask a question, Doctor? I mean a real question, not one of those prodding things you toss in once in a while just to prove that you're earning your money or that you haven't gone to sleep. Don't answer me now. I know. A real question contains always its own answer. I am my own interrogator here. You are simply a tape recorder with a medical education. But isn't thirty dollars an hour high rent for a tape recorder, even with all those degrees?

Very well, Doctor Fowler, I will stop playing the fool and get back to the business of dredging up the muck of my life, in honor of St. Sigmund and St. Alfred and St. Carl Gustav the Junger and good St. Karen.

Before I married, you mean? Oh yes, I tried. Of course I tried. It seemed to me humiliating to have no sex life at the age of twenty-one. Humiliating and abnormal and very bad form. So I tried. When I was at Bryn Mawr I went for a weekend with a Princeton boy to a place in the Poconos. I wore a dime store ring and we registered as Mr. and Mrs. All very matter of fact. Grown up stuff, you see. We had dinner in front of the fire and two drinks each in the bar and then we went upstairs to the big warm rustic room. I was not afraid. I was dispassionate as a trained nurse bathing a man in his bed. It is not a thing one can hide. The poor boy was terrified. We got into the bed and he kissed me. His hand touched my breast; it was cold as ice on my skin. For a long time we lay there in the dark room that had been hired for sin. Outside were the sounds of creatures in the woods, the sound of an automobile horn far off on the highway. "I am sorry," he said. "I don't know what is the matter." "It is all right," I said. Under the sheets, in the dark, my hand moved and touched his impotence, shocked by the limp insignificance of it. It was a cruel thing to do. He moved in the bed as if he had been stabbed and cried out like a hurt child: "Don't! Don't do that please!" I smiled in the darkness and touched him no more. In the night, in the bed beside me, he was a symbol of something or other:—the helpless, flaccid male, the warrior conquered before he fought. In the morning he was the symbol of nothing, but only an innocent Princeton boy with a short haircut and nice manners, filled with delicate apologies.

How he must have hated me!

Try, they say, and try again. Once I tried with an older man. I had read up on the subject, you see. He was an English actor with beautiful grey temples and an ascot scarf in regimental colors. That effort stopped after some kissing on the couch. "Would you like to sleep with me?" I asked.

You see, it was my apartment.

He gave me his regimental smile and straightened his regimental ascot. "Really, my dear," he said. "I don't think it would be worth the effort for either of us."

By that time I was twenty-two and beginning to realize that there was something about me sexually that was quite, quite wrong. Yet it was a thing I wanted. It was something I had tasted during those four days in Maine and I wanted more of it. And it was something you were supposed to have, for health's sake and pleasure's and on general principles.

I tried brutality once with a soldier, or was he a marine?

At any rate he was quite direct. He did not remove his khaki socks and during the blitzkrieg—I don't think the whole performance took more than three minutes—he kept saying "Oh baby! Oh baby! What am I givin' to you, baby?" He hit me hard on the mouth when I would not answer him. Then he hit me again, with his fist. "Cock, baby. Hard cock. That's what I'm a-givin' you." With which he was finished. He put on his shirt and pants, took a bottle of my whiskey, and walked out of my apartment. I went to the bathroom and was sick, on my knees by the toilet bowl.

After the paratrooper—that's what he was—I decided to experiment no more. Other people talked about sex in very serious terms. It was a means of communication, the one that worked where language failed. It bridged classes. It was symbolic—giving, receiving, etcetera, etcetera, etcetera. For me it was meaningless, baffling as the idea of color must be baffling to a man born blind. By the time I went to Hollywood I thought of myself as a sexual cripple, a kind of female eunuch. I read all the popular books on the subject by all the popular psychiatrists. I learned nothing but some terminology. Penis envy! That's not what I yearned for at all. I yearned for nothing. I did not burn with desire. I simply was conscious of a lack in myself, awareness that something had been left out. Something had not been put in. And there I was with a diaphragm that had been fitted by the most expensive pessary-fitter in Beverly Hills. Poor little rich girl!

I found that matters were somewhat different when I had taken enough to drink. It was a thing I discovered by accident. I went to one of those parties on the alcoholic littoral of somebody's swimming pool. There were jeraboams of champagne in ice buckets mounted on wheels, little champagne wagons they were, silently rolled from guest to guest by doll-like Japanese servants. When the party began, as I remember, most of us wore bathing suits. Later on most of us seemed to have taken them off. There were a great many people and lots of movement and loud laughter. Piped music came from a dozen miniature loud speakers hidden in the potted palm trees. I sat naked on the edge of the pool, trailing my feet in the costly water, drinking champagne. When it is cold and of the best quality, champagne is easy to drink. The bubbles went up my nose again, just the way they had at the Lodge on my birthday and I became quite merry. I don't know how much I had to drink but it was enough to make me draw a blank. My first, mind you, but not my last. When I came out of the blank I thought I was struggling with an animal in a kind of halfdream. Then I realized that I was in one of the cabanas, in bed with a well-known cowboy actor, whose well-known face and well-known shoulders loomed above me in the dusky light. He was making love to me very slowly, very tenderly, his body moving lazily as one of those huge fans African house boys use in films. He was a boy who had taken lessons, this ersatz cowhand inside of me. I pretended to respond and discovered that I could manage in a mechanical kind of way. I don't mean that my performance would have qualified me as a high-priced whore, but he seemed to be fooled. Certainly he was not rendered impotent by my coldness, the way most of the others had been.

When he had finished with me he stood up and switched on the light so that I could see what I had been privileged to enjoy. He was like one of those ads for a muscle-building course, so tall that his head nearly touched the ceiling of the cabana. His skin was brown as a Polynesian's, startling with his straw-colored hair. He lit a cigarette and handed it to me and said that he thought it was quite a party. He spoke with a southwestern accent, exactly as he did in his pictures. It was legitimate; actually he had been a cowhand on a big ranch in Texas, though he herded cattle in a jeep then, not on trusty old Ponto.

We finished our cigarettes and went back to the swimming pool and put on our bathing suits. The night was dark and smog-free. There was an enormous Hollywood moon. Across the pool on a patio that covered nearly an acre, tiny lights winked and moved. They were the lights on the champagne wagons. On the dark side of the pool, where we stood in the moonlight, naked couples were locked together in the liquid shadows. The love making seemed to be over. No one moved or made a sound. My mouth was dry and I asked for a drink. The cowboy commandeered a wagon and filled two glasses. I held the fragile glass in my hand, watching the moonlight on the bubbles. I am grateful to you, I thought, touching the glass with my lips. This muscleman may not have given me quite the pleasure he thinks he did but at least, thanks to you, I was able to behave more or less the way that other kindly girls behave when they are in bed with a man.

"You sure are a pretty girl, Miss McBride," the cowboy said at that moment, in his rawhide accent. "I don't know when I've enjoyed pleasurin' myself so much."

He drove me home in an enormous cream-colored car that he told me was a Ferrari. He left me in the driveway of the little house the studio had rented for me, making no move to come in. Off he went in his absurd car, creating a little storm of gravel. I went into the house slowly. The drive in the night had cleared my head. My God! I thought, when I was in my bedroom getting ready to take a bath, suppose that great big adorable hunk of man has gotten me pregnant with his great big adorable instrument that had not quite done the trick for me? What on earth will I do with a miniature cowhand? I filled the douche-bag with hot water and loaded the water with lysol, scalding my insides. I knew the douche was no good really, but I had to do something.

Nothing happened. I was edgy for two weeks and irritable on the set but I came around all right. After that I put on my costly diaphragm whenever I went to a party where there would be a lot of drinking. Not that very much happened. Sometimes when I'd had enough to drink I would go to bed with a man. My sexual manners were better than they had been back east but that was all there was to it; courtesy on my part. I made no alliances for more than a night. I never had an orgasm. I have not experienced one since the episode at the Lodge. I remember a phrase from a book. "Certain people are unable to love or to inspire love." That's me! I remember saying, when I encountered the phrase on the page. That's little old Carlotta. Unable to love or inspire love.

But it was not quite true.

I found that out when we were making my third picture, the one that pushed my salary up high enough for people to notice. That was *Breakdown*. Perhaps you've seen it. Almost everyone has, I guess. It nearly killed me, that picture. I wish I had never made it.

—Most of *Breakdown* was made on location at the Desert State Hospital, otherwise known as the loony bin. It is a fantastic place. It looks like a State university except that there are steel grilles at the windows of most of the buildings. There are great lawns, beautifully shorn, and lots of winding leafy lanes with stone benches where the patients sit in the pure brilliant sunlight, those who aren't locked up behind the grilled windows. It is a beautiful place and there is nothing to criticize, yet even outside the buildings on the broad subsections of expensive grass it is a place where the air itself seems to be charged with fear. One feels vague, free-floating discomfort, then tension, then the urge to turn and run. Perhaps it is actually in the air. Perhaps the disturbed or shattered minds, thousands of them, harboring behind the green-grown walls, themselves give off a potent charge, like static electricity.

We had a pedantic Hungarian director who had known Freud in Vienna. He was determined to make a picture about madness that would be a commercial success but that must also be authentic to the last Rorschach blot. His belief in study was profound. For three weeks we did no shooting at all but simply lived in the hospital, soaking up the atmosphere. We took our meals in a dining hall reserved for the less disturbed patients. We talked with doctors and orderlies and nurses and patients.

It was a very unsettling experience and I'm not at all sure that it helped the film.

It was a teaching hospital and there were certain curious rooms fitted with panels made of one-way glass, so that without being seen it was possible to observe patients undergoing electric shock, massive sedation, hydro-therapy, chemical hypnosis, things like that. I first saw my husband in that way, through a glass darkly, as you might say.

You have seen his photograph.

What is really impressive about him is the aroma of competence and that doesn't show very much in the photograph. Watching him through the trick glass, listening to his voice that came through the hidden mikes, I had the feeling that here perhaps was the one man on the face of this earth who actually knew what he was doing. His patient was a young woman being prepared for shock therapy, a creature in deep depression, slack-mouthed, her eyes vacant, a being almost no longer human. I was fascinated, watching him handle this woman bereft of normal responses, with kindness but very effectively, so that while there was no brutality, no time was lost. When the treatment was over I waited for him at the door of the room with the trick window. He looked at me disinterestedly. I was wearing a long white coat and might have been a doctor or a laboratory technician. Then he noticed my shoes and said, "Oh, you are one of the movie people." I gathered he didn't approve of the idea of permitting outsiders to have more or less free run of a mental hospital. We walked down the corridor together and I asked him if he would not like to have a cup of coffee with me. He hesitated, then looked at me, seeming to see me for the first time. "Yes. Yes, that would be nice," he said. We went to the staff canteen and drank black bitter coffee from heavy hospital mugs. We talked. As we sat over the coffee his clannish reserve fell away. He was a very young man, hardly older than I was then, and very much a doctor, one of those professionals who has worked hard at one thing from the age of ten or eleven, living a life that centered on a single idea, almost an ascetic yet not quite, for there was warmth in him and a sense of humor. He liked me; I made him laugh.

That night, after eating my dinner in the hall filled with madmen and women, I sat on the edge of the bed in my room, staring at a cheap print on the innocuous green wall, deciding, as if I were deciding to take a part in a play, that I was going to marry Doctor Ericson. And marry him I did. I am an actress and a good one. We were on location for six weeks, in the hospital every day. I was the outside world to him, bright, amusing and attractive. By the time we had finished shooting he was in love with me. A week after we left the desert he drove to Hollywood to see me. Three weeks later we were married and on the way to Paris.

That was all there was to the marriage, those four weeks in Paris. I had been able to fool the cowboy and certain casual others but I couldn't fool him no matter how much champagne I'd had to drink before we got into bed. He was in love with me, you see, or at least he was in love with the character I had been playing. He wanted to make love to me, to be romantic, impassioned, to take me to bed in the afternoon in the big hotel in Paris, with the french windows wide open, the smell of the trees coming into the room and the sound of traffic on the Champs Eliseés.

I did not want him to love me. I wanted him to cure me, as he had tried to cure the catatonic patient in the shock therapy room. It was not a valid idea. I wanted him to heal my wounds, but I did not intend to let him see them or to tell him anything at all about the symptoms of my illness, if it is an illness that I have and not simply an Irish curse. I lied to him as I have lied to so many, many other people. I told him my father had been killed in the war and that since his death my sainted and dearly beloved mother had become a recluse. I told him I was Irish and Catholic and pretended that my doubts about God were real.

I wanted him to cure me but I was not his patient. I was his wife according to the laws of the State of California and he was not practicing medicine in that hotel room in Paris on those bright afternoons.

It was cruel of me to marry him, and dishonest. Before we were married he had stayed for the weekend in my rented, bastard Spanish house. I had the sense of playing a part from the moment he arrived, as if the lines had been put down for me by a skillful and corrupted writer who had adapted them from somebody else's book. It was the same at night in my bed, with the moon shadow of a palm tree falling across the silk sheets that came with the rented house. I went through the motions of the act of love like a tutored and high-priced whore. I felt nothing. I have read somewhere that in India, (or is it Persia?) men read books or play solitaire while they are making love, in order to hold back and to compensate for the slower pace of their wives. It is not a sound practice for the female of the species.

I knew that night in California that there was no chance for us at all, yet I did not break it off. He had no way of knowing the truth. He simply assumed that I was not ready and in the morning, at breakfast on my patio, he asked me to marry him. I suspect that I have no conscience. I accepted the proposal without bothering to tell him that he was acquiring imperfect merchandise.

We never quarreled in Paris. Sometimes I think my mind would be easier if we had fought, even fought with our fists, if he had denounced me for being a fraud, called me dirty names, kicked me in the stomach. We did not fight. We passed four weeks together in Paris and at the end of the time we were strangers. On the last afternoon, when we were packing our bags to come home, I think we were more completely strangers than we had been the day we met in the hospital corridor, outside the shock therapy room. Then at least there had been no lies between us, spoken or unspoken.

He returned to his madhouse in the desert. I went back to the studio to make another picture. It was the arrangement we had made when we married, because it was important for him to finish his residency and impossible for me to live in the desert. He did not come back to me. When his time was up at the hospital, he wrote me a letter and told me that he had taken an appointment at a hospital in San Juan, Puerto Rico. Nothing had been said, yet everything had been stated. The divorce was mechanical, arranged by a studio lawyer, impersonal as a lawsuit over a smashed fender where neither driver is to be blamed. It was after the divorce that the sense of failure struck me, sharp, challenging awareness of inadequacy and guilt. How much I hurt him I don't know, but I know how much I hurt myself.

It was my first nose dive with alcohol. I could not shake off the depression or rid myself of the sense of emptiness, the conviction that I was nothing, that I was no more really than the slab-faced patient in an unironed nightgown that he had put through electric shock. I could make responses but they were not my own. On the sound stage, under the bright lights, I acted out responses that had been written down for me and when I was not in front of the cameras I went on acting. I felt as though I had been laced into a canvas straitjacket or put into some kind of trance by means of a vicious, malevolent drug. I began to drink, deliberately, in the middle of making a picture, with the idea that somehow I could drink my way out of my prison. Once started I discovered that I had a positive gift for drinking. And for a time it seemed to work. At least I was moving, I was not sitting on a hard bench like the girl in the shock room.

I went to bars and to people's houses, to swimming pool parties and to low dives, to slick places in Los Angeles where one encounters fashionable gangsters. I went home with various men and sometimes with various women. I brought others home with me. Drunk almost to the point of black-out but still on my feet, still talking and walking, I was able to inhabit a sexual slum and to be used as a sexual sewer seemed appropriate punishment for whatever it was I had done.

Hollywood has a large population of well-known sexual athletes, men and women who operate singly or in groups. I was a kind of census taker during those weeks after the divorce, when I was trying to find out how much Irish whiskey a young woman can consume without actually dying. Some Anglo-Irish critic has said that the extended drunk is a minor work of art, a creative act in which the materials of art dissolve. I understand what he means. On a binge there is a kind of form to be observed. And the drinking itself takes on the character of an obligation. "Got to go down to the village tonight and get drunk and God how I dread it," the old farmer is supposed to have said. It is true. One has loyalty to the ritual. I was a novice in those weeks but I had money and there were lots of people willing to teach me the rules of the game. I was a quick student or perhaps it was just beginner's luck.

The studio suspended me and sent various emissaries to plead, threaten, bully and cajole. Then they hired a pair of private detectives to keep tabs on me, a man and woman who followed me everywhere I went. One night when I passed out in a bad bar in L.A. they kidnapped me, pretending to be friends of mine kind enough to take me home. I woke up two days later in a nursing home, filled with barbiturates, my backside still sore from the hypodermic needles. It was a pretty room with screens at the window that couldn't be moved. For a moment I thought I had gone to sleep in somebody's spare bedroom. There was a nice rug on the floor, a chair covered in soft tan leather, pictures on the walls. Then I felt the soreness in my buttocks and realized that I wore a nightgown of the kind that hospitals use. I was furious. I did not want anyone, even God Almighty, to do anything for me for my own good. My own good was my own and I was god damned if I was not going to take care of it myself.

The rest of that story I suppose almost everyone knows, everyone, that is, who reads the tabloids and the picture magazines. I walked out of the nursing home barefoot, wearing nothing but the nightgown that buttoned up the back and didn't button well enough to keep my behind covered. There was no reason in me, only rage, literally blinding rage. As I stumbled down hill from the big house I was so mad I could hardly see. The only thing I understood was that I meant to get away.

I stood on the highway and hitch-hiked south. Don't tell me that certain meetings aren't arranged for us in heaven or in hell. The first car that came along pulled to the side of the road and picked me up. The driver was a big good-natured man who wore a cream-colored silk shirt. The car was almost new, a Ford, the newspapers said later, though to me it looked more impressive and larger than a Ford should be. "Climb aboard," the driver said, leaning over to open the door. When I got in he looked at me and whistled. "Left some place in a hurry, didn't you?" he said, putting the car back in gear and stepping on the gas. "I'm not an escaped lunatic," I said. "I ran away from a very exclusive drying-out place for drunks, on account of I didn't think I was ready to be dried out quite yet." He laughed and put his foot on the brake, pulled to the right and brought the car to a stop on the shoulder of the road. He rummaged in the back seat of the car and found a shirt and a pair of pants. "Belong to my daughter," he said. "But I guess they'll fit after a fashion. Go over behind that billboard and put 'em on, before we get ourselves arrested." I took the things from him and went behind the billboard. I stripped off the hospital gown and stood naked in the warm sun. Then I put on the shirt and pants. It was a G.I. shirt and the pants were blue jeans that had been boiled until they were faded and soft, the way teen-age kids liked them.

When I got back to the car the man grinned at me and said, "That's better. I don't mind myself but other people might think it was funny to see you riding around in your night shirt." I got into the car, leaning back in the seat. "My God I need a drink," I said. "Happens you've come to the right place," he said. "I sell the stuff. Drink it too, though maybe I shouldn't." He opened the glove compartment and took out a bottle of bonded bourbon, unscrewing the cap and handing it to me. I drank from the bottle, paused, then drank again. It was very good bourbon, smooth almost as sherry, with a lovely winey undertaste. I thanked him and returned the bottle. He took a goodsized swig then put the bottle away. "It's there when you want it," he said. "Don't have to ask permission." He started the car and swung back onto the highway, then asked me where I was heading. "Anywhere," I told him. "You've got the right driver," he said. "That's where I go, anywhere. Anywhere in southern California." I told him I didn't have any money but that I could get some by telegram. "Who asked you for money?" he said. "Sit back and relax."

He was a drinking man and a gentleman. I stood on the edge of the road almost naked and the first car that came along carried a drinking man who was a gentleman. It might have been a policeman or a murderer or a Protestant minister or a man who enjoyed raping women or burning their feet with cigarettes, but it was none of these that had stopped his car and picked me up.

He was a systematic drinker who needed no more than a stroke of luck to start him on a binge. I was his stroke of luck. He liked me at once and I liked him. I trusted him. Not for an instant, from the moment he handed me his daughter's shirt and pants, did it occur to me that I was in the slightest danger from him. Danger of anything, I mean, even of a harsh word.

At nightfall we stopped at a colony of tourist cabins, a nice place that he knew, with good beds and clean toilets. He unlocked the trunk of his car and took out four bottles of whiskey, bringing them into the cabin. Neither of us wanted to eat. We sat on the edge of the narrow cots on either side of the cabin and drank straight whiskey out of the plastic tooth glasses that came from the rack in the bright clean toilet. We talked easily about nothing, the way people can talk when they drink. He told me how he peddled liquor all over southern California, how he had gone into the business because, being a drinking man himself, he knew that liquor was the last thing people will give up, if they really use it at all. "They'll go hungry and cold," he told me, "and wear raggedy shirts and worn down heels, but they'll still get up the price of a bottle." Once, after several hours of drinking, he sat on the edge of my bed and put a hand on my breast. "No," I said, knowing that it would be all right. He got up and went back to his own cot. "Just thought you might be put out if I didn't try," he said. "Some women are that way."

He was a wonderful man, gentle and kind and hopeless, with a kind of intuitive grace about him, a carefulness never to offend. When he used the toilet he made it a point to be as quiet as possible. When I used it, he went outside and stood at the door of the cabin until he had heard the john flush and knew that I was finished.

We stayed in the cabin for three days, drinking steadily, once in a while eating part of a soggy hamburger cooked by the motel man. It was the kind of drinking in which one sets up a private universe in microcosm. All our needs were satisfied in that little room which was perhaps ten feet by twelve. From time to time he went to the car to get more liquor. From time to time we used the phone to order the soggy hamburgers. From time to time and without regard to the hour of the day or night, one or the other of us would stretch out on his cot and sleep, for ten minutes, twenty, two hours at the longest. It is a wonderful kind of world, a marvelous alcoholic womb, warm and safe, constant, undemanding.

On the morning of the fourth day he shaved for the first time, going to the car for his bag, which he had not bothered to carry into the cabin the day we arrived. He told me he had to get moving. "Got to sell a little whiskey for a change, instead of trying to drink it all," he said gently.

I used his comb and scrubbed the inside of my mouth with toothpaste on my finger. I splashed cold water on my face and rubbed the skin dry, then realized that my hands were filthy. How did I get so dirty? I wondered. The room is clean. The car was clean. In four days I haven't touched anything except those nice clean bottles. Nevertheless, my hands were dirty as if I had been shoveling coal. *"Les Mains Sales,"* I said, rolling up the sleeves of my borrowed shirt and turning on the hot water. *"La Putain Respectueuse."* I scrubbed my hands with his nail brush, singing to myself: "I've got that Sartre'n feelin'." I was very drunk, so drunk that ever being sober again seemed absurdly impossible. Yet my mind functioned with a false clarity that made me seem brilliant and very witty and I made my companion laugh when we were back on the road. He was delighted with me even when my jokes were bad or puns like the one about Sartre that he couldn't understand.

It was a bright clear day with just a bit of haze on the horizon, a beautiful day for driving. We started south toward San Diego, traveling at high speed, seventy, eighty miles an hour, burning up the long straight road. It was thrilling. The awareness of speed was absolute. "How fast will it go?" I said, my hair whipping at my cheeks, my eyes smarting a little. "Faster than this," he said. He took a drink from the glove compartment bottle, guiding the car with one hand, but pretty steadily, then pressed the gas pedal to the floor. The speedometer needle began to climb, easily at first then with some reluctance. "Ninety-six, ninety-seven," he said, counting, his eyes on the needle. "Ninety-eight... nine... a hundred!"

The car trembled like a frightened animal but he held it to speed. I saw the truck before he did and I think I tried to scream. An instant later we hit it and the car turned over, then seemed to bounce and turned again. We were in the ditch. I was badly cut on the arms by glass from the windshield but I was conscious and I didn't think I was badly hurt. He was dead. He had tried to duck at the moment we hit and his skull had been smashed. I sat beside him in the car, drenched with whiskey. The reek was incredible. When we hit the truck most of the bottles he carried in the trunk had been smashed. I tried to get out of the car but the door was wedged shut. I opened the glove compartment. That bottle had not been broken. I sat there sipping from it until I heard the sirens of the patrol car. I could see the car on the bank above me, signal lights flashing. Then there were two highway patrolmen on motorcycles. For several seconds the four policemen stood on the verge of the road where the guard-rail had been torn away by the car. They were like soldiers on parade, belted and booted, heavy pistols on their thighs. "Holy-Mary-Mother-of-God!" I heard one of them say. Then they came down the bank, sideways, like mountaineers, slipping a little in the soft shale. They lifted me out of the lacerated car and took the bottle away from me.

"Give it back," I said. "It's mine."

The policeman was a tall young man with blond hair cropped short. "No, lady," he said. "You had enough."

I fought with him for the bottle. He used one hand, trying not to hurt me, holding the bottle in the other. It slipped from his fingers and fell, the glass smashing on a rock. I sat on the ground and began to wail: "Now look what you've done. Now look what you've done. You broke my bottle. You broke my bottle."

They carried me up the embankment and lifted me into the radio car. One of them held my hands all the way to the police barracks, holding them quite gently, the way a man might hold the hands of a child to prevent him from doing something dangerous.

The studio had sent out an alarm for me the day before and at the barracks one of the policemen recognized me. "You're crazy," another one said. "Did you see the sneak preview of *Breakdown?*" the first one asked. "The part where she runs away from the loony bin? Take another look, pal." All of them inspected me critically and after a little they were agreed that I was Carlotta McBride. Then there were reporters and photographers and after a while a lawyer and two press agents, emissaries of the studio, members of the Praetorian Guard. The lawyer arranged things with the police. The two men from the publicity department argued one with the other. "There might be an angle," one of them said. "There just might be an angle."

I suppose that photograph of me wearing the G.I. shirt and blue jeans, barefoot, blood on my face, must have been reproduced in at least a thousand newspapers and magazines. I am told that prints were bootlegged and pasted to the mirrors in the back-bars of saloons. I never saw one. The photograph, someone told me, was worth a million dollars to the studio. The public liked it. What should have been bad, even fatal publicity, turned out to be a gold mine. It was because of *Breakdown,* you see. People thought of me as mad—bright, brave, brittle, and mad—so naturally they were pleased when in real life I behaved like a madwoman. I am told there is a French girl who is in fact a virgin but who has been turned into a kind of international trollop by the publicity people. At any rate, that picture and the stories that went with it, turned *Breakdown* into a smash. There were even those knowledgeable people who insisted that the whole thing was a publicity stunt, except that the man had-died by mistake.

Certainly he had died. I went to his funeral in a little town outside San Francisco. The church was Catholic and forlorn, with a tin steeple painted red to match the brick of the building. The priest was a middleaged man, disenchanted and detached. I sat in the church and listened to the Latin, wishing my friend could have had somehow a funeral better suited to his temperament. But perhaps I was wrong. At the cemetery his wife stood beside me when the grave was being covered. She was a small woman with a sweet, tired face, pale eyes, pale hair, everything about her pale except the stiff new black of the weeds she was wearing. "I am sorry," I said. She had written to me and asked me to come but this was the first we had spoken. "It wasn't your fault," she said. "He was a good man but he drank too much. He didn't need anybody to lead him astray, so don't blame yourself for what happened to him. Sooner or later it would have happened anyhow." She looked at me curiously. I was dressed in a black suit and a simple black hat. I suppose I looked attractive. "Did he go to sleep with you, when he was on that binge?" she asked. I shook my head. "I was afraid not," she said. "He never cared much for that, when he was drinking. But it would have been something for him, I suppose, you being a movie star and all." I think I began to cry then. I stumbled away from the grave, over the grass in my high heels, toward the steel barred gate where a car was waiting for me. I sat in the back of the limousine driving toward Los Angeles, humiliated, angry at her. "She has no right not to hate me," I thought. "She has no right not to slap my face, curse me, kill me, even."

But of course she had the right. Without knowing what she did, with a great deal of gentleness, she had put a wound in my heart, so that for a long time I was like a person who has been submitted to cardiac surgery, heart laid bare and cut open, then sewed up again, functioning, but making a fatal response to any forbidden movement or tabued exertion. She had added him, and permanently, to the roster of my guilt. He is still there. Harry Simpson. I did not know his last name until after he was dead.

The studio put me back on salary and I finished the picture we had been making when my nose dive began. I thought it was a very bad picture indeed but it made a great deal of money. After *Breakdown* I suppose anything with me in it would have made money, even a short subject on the flora of the desert.

That summer I did a TV series on film.

The studio sent me scripts to read, great fat greasy scripts with stories I cared nothing about. I would have made one or the other of them out of sheer boredom, except that Falkstein sent me this play to read and I came east to do it. The play was written for me, you see. I didn't really like it but the idea of being on a real stage, in front of an audience, appealed to me, and I was bored with the West Coast.

I wasn't drinking heavily. Shock therapy, you see, Doctor, but a very difficult technique, involving the use of an actual corpse. For a long time after the smash-up I found it impossible to get drunk, though it wasn't the smash-up that intervened but the pale woman in the cemetery who was sorry her husband had been too drunk to get into bed with a movie star.

I took the apartment I live in now and began to catch up with New York. I was almost happy, I never really liked the Coast. New York is my home town. While we were rehearsing I used to go to Fourth Avenue in the mornings, looking at second-hand books and sometimes buying one. Just south of the bookshops is the Bowery. The alcoholics drift uptown to panhandle at the open stalls that stand in front of the bookshops. One morning, in the distance, I saw a man begging. With a book in my hand I watched him, caught by something familiar in his silhouette, the way he moved as he made his plea to a passerby, then another. I put the book back on the stand and walked toward the man who begged. It was Daddy, I was sure, dressed in shapeless flophouse clothes, unshaven, unkempt. I called out to him. He turned, swaying a little, saw me and turned away. I walked toward him. He began to run, turning a corner. I ran after him. He could not run very far. I found him in a doorway, gasping for his breath, exhausted by the few seconds exertion. I sat in the doorway beside him and touched his arm. He looked up at me, eyes filled with hurt. It was not Michael McBride but only a man who resembled him.

"I am sorry," I said. "I thought you were someone else."

"Lady, I am someone else," he said.

I gave him a five dollar bill. He got to his feet awkwardly and lurched away toward the Bowery, toward the alcoholic swamp of flophouses and damp alleys and dreadful bars and shops that keep wine on ice.

"Where is he?" I asked myself. "Is he alive or dead?"

When I had thought about him I had seen him in comfortable tragic exile, sitting in a beach chair alone with his sadness, pining with hopeless love for me. But he had always been a drinking man and drink was something I understood now as I had not when I was a child. Perhaps he is like that man, I thought, matted and filthy, helpless with drink, homeless and begging on the street.

For a long time I had pushed him down into the bottom of my mind, where he remained like a piece of valuable but forgotten jewelry. Now he had come to the surface and I was smashed with guilt and shame and struck by the sense of rejection.

"I cannot bear it," I said, raising my hands to my ears as if to shut out some dreadful sound. "This I cannot bear."

There was a saloon on the corner. I plunged through the door and stood at the bar. "Whiskey," I said. "Irish whiskey."

I told Falkstein that I was ill and that he would have to stop rehearsals. I drank for a month at Sheridan's Bar on Third Avenue. I became an habitué. It is astonishing how quickly you become an habitué of Sheridan's if Sheridan decides he approves of you. It is a little world, a little kingdom, isolated and preserved in drink. The room is narrow, perhaps twelve feet wide from wall to wall. There are booths in the back, a scabrous linoleum floor, a reeking kerosene heater, toilets that smell like those in a French village. The walls and the back bar are covered with memorabilia of the war and the Irish revolution, German helmets, an SS officer's dirk, a shilaleagh, a bit of bright green ribbon said to have been worn on Easter Week, dozens of photographs of well-known people, all inscribed to Sheridan Himself. There is a photograph of me, framed and hung near the cash register. Over everything except the bar itself is a layer of grease and dust, so that walls and pictures and posters and whatnot seemed to have been subjected to some inexpert flocking process, coating them with a fine oily fuzz. The bar and glasses and bottles are clean and so is Sheridan himself clean.

It is a world with its own rhythm, its own gossip, its own economic fluctuations, its own rivalries and romances, its own system of love and hate…a drunkard's village, compressed in size, fitted into a narrow room, governed by a thin-faced Irish king with a gift for talk and a weakness for drink.

I became a part of that world during that month that dropped out of time, and I lived with reference to it. My friends were there: Arthur the Artist; Beauregard Johnson, the professional gentleman; a Princeton man who earned his living teaching the blind to walk and spent it trying to become blind in front of Sheridan's bar. There was the Duchess—there is always a Duchess, in bars like this one—and there was Fat Mabel, the waitress, and there was Kathleen, who had once been within a single vote of becoming Miss America. There was Big Panther, the mountainous Negro, and Lou-Lou Holland, who had once upon a time been welterweight champion of the world. There was Juicy Ryan, handyman from a big apartment house, and there was George Gordon Byron Spolato, a synthetic Englishman who wore the ties of half a dozen schools and regiments and drank on all of them. These were the regulars. There were others, the occasionals, Hollywood people on the loose, writers, press agents, advertising people, a collaboration from The Players on Gramercy Park. It is a world with its own decorum, protocol tight as a private club. After a little I became a member and now I am always safe there. After all, Dr. Fowler, one has rights in his own house.

Why did I leave my own house then? I was happy that month in Sheridan's in a way that people who do not drink will never understand. I preferred the time scheme there to the one we use in the outside world and it is a society in which one moves without too much subterfuge because all of it is subterfuge. I like the people. They are my friends—Sheridan himself, Arthur the Artist, even the scrawny and awful Duchess. Why did I not go back to Sheridan's when they signed me out of the hospital?

Fear, my friend. Fear of drink. Fear of the creature that lives in the bottle.

The chemistry of drinking is imprecise. Sometimes the effect cannot be predicted, yet this should be so. This many ounces of alcohol, this many ounces of blood in the body, such and such a physical state. It should be a matter as simple as giving ether to a patient or pouring dye into a vat and knowing the cloth will come out a certain color. Whiskey, alcohol, they tell me, is an anesthetic, but it is not well behaved. Trying to outguess whiskey is somewhat the same as forecasting the weather. There are rules that govern the weather's behavior but sometimes the weather ignores the rules and follows its own caprice. The weather is whimsical. So is whiskey.

I went to Sheridan's saloon one afternoon, an ordinary afternoon in October, pleasantly cool, quite clear, the kind of day that inspires conversation with strangers. I had been drinking for about a month and the drinking itself had imposed a kind of routine upon my life, inexorable as the demand of a school or a job or the practice of an art. Drinking in this way becomes an occupation. During that month I got up every day more or less at noon and took a long time to dress—two hours, perhaps, if one includes the long soapy shower. With my coffee I drank a Bloody Mary or sometimes an Americano. I read the paper or tried to read it while I emerged from my hangover. People who drink occasionally have no conception of the hangover as we initiates understand and love it. Once upon a time Mr. Auden wrote a letter to his wound. Better burn this, he says at the end. It is a love letter. The hangover is a pampered wound, a well-loved affliction, dear as a child's small cut adorned with a bright new band-aid. It is an affliction that commands tender and studied attention. And it is enjoyable. I know. But don't say it. Don't tell me it is a matter of guilt that welcomes the punishing pain. That, my dear Dr. Fowler, is shit. The hangover is a thing in itself, beloved because it is part of the drunk, part of the wonderful continuum that is sensed on a long drunk, the sense of being caught and held and borne weightless through time, drifting without weight in a river with a single current, floating through time until at last the always slower alcoholic clock runs down, so that the movement of the hands is imperceptible and there is no time, there is no place, but only an environment, a cocoon that one inhabits, taking the foetal position on the stool in a bar, alone though surrounded by people, silent though endlessly talking, insensitive even to the pain of fire, beyond the giving or receiving of insult; alive, though dead.

On that October afternoon I had two Bloody Marys and read the *Times* straight through to the shipping news and reports of fires. At a little after two I took my shower, soaping myself again and again, not to wash away the guilt, my friend, but because I loved the voluptuous sensation of stroking my body, when it had been lathered with soap that was deliciously perfumed.

When I finished my bath I dressed myself with some care. I have not yet succumbed to the temptation to go into the street in slacks or blue jeans, or to put on the clothes of the night before, simply because they are on the chair or the floor and the maid hasn't had a chance to shake them out and put them away. I wore a good brown dress that day, made of soft French tweed, a dress I liked and wore well. I put on a gold necklace and earrings and a thin gold bracelet. I remember slipping into a pair of Italian shoes, beautiful things made of brown lizard. The paper had said that it would be forty degrees. I put on my mink coat. I had a bag to match the shoes and I put a hundred dollars into the silk change purse, new ten dollar bills from the bank, crisp and sharp enough to cut your finger, lovely bright new drinking money. I always kept cash in the drawer of my desk, five or six hundred dollars, so that there wouldn't be the bother of forever cashing checks.

I reached Sheridan's at about three-thirty. Con Malone was behind the bar, round-faced, intelligent, grey-haired before his time. Sheridan himself works at night. On a stool sat Arthur the Artist, one hand guarding his qualifying beer, the half-filled glass that gave him the right to occupy a stool and a few feet of Sheridan's air. I bought Arthur a double vodka, then another, and we talked about art. Most of what I know about painting I have learned from Arthur the Artist. He reads very much, and when he is not in Sheridan's he is at the Met or in one of the commercial galleries. His judgments are sound and better constructed than those of people who write about art for the papers and magazines. You think I am joking or deceiving myself but please, Dr. Fowler, be certain that I am not. Arthur is no painter, surely, but he understands these things. We sat drinking: double vodka, double whiskey, double vodka, double whiskey, talking about art.

Sometime later Beauregard Johnson joined us. Over his arm he carried a suit just bought in the Thrift Shop. He showed me the London label and I admired the buttonholes at the cuff and agreed with him when he pointed out that a decent tailor always takes especial care with these buttonholes that are never used. The crew of a moving van came in and very courteously insisted upon buying me a drink. Silently as a colorless eel the Duchess took up her position at the very end of the bar. Silently too, old Pat Keeley sipped whiskey mixed with milk and got on with his dying. A beer salesman took an order and bought drinks for all. Con Malone, when he was not busy, rested an arm on the back bar and sourly contemplated the street, naked now without the El.

It was an afternoon at Sheridan's, exactly like dozens of other afternoons. I was drinking whiskey quite slowly, whiskey diluted with water and ice. Beyond the unwashed window pane the other world went about its business. In the saloon we sat in safety, lapped in the timeless dimension of whiskey, tolerant each one of the other, luxuriously private, self-contained. In the other world the pleasures of narcissism are an embarrassment and one is obliged to give them disguises. The drunkard is frankly concerned with himself, egocentric as an infant sucking his own thumb. A trained alcoholic at certain moments is sufficient unto himself. He will regard with fascination the beauty of his own hand, the unique texture of his sleeve, the exquisite curve of the arch of his foot. Euphoria. Someone who has studied the matter suggests that this alcoholic balance, hard-sought but never sustained, is similar to what one felt as an infant suckling at the breast. Perhaps. Certainly it involves the illusion of being held close and warm and safe. Sometimes Irish people call a public house a "snug." "I'm just goin' down the street now, Mary, to get a drink at McCarthy's snug." It is a good word.

The warmth we seek and the rest we need.

There is something in the air of Sheridan's bar that extends this measure of borrowed peace, which is always of course on loan and always snatched away.

At six o'clock on that October evening Sheridan came into the bar and the tempo changed at once. There was a sharpening of interest, a sense of anticipation—the star's entrance, the main event, the horses all at the starting post. It was Sheridan superbly sober, exactly as advertised from here to Hollywood—Sheridan the wit, the host and the arbitrator, canon of the dark cathedral, dispenser of life, physician and friend, good Catholic husband and father, interpreter of Shaun the Post, infallible pope of the dogma of drink, chairman of the board of the club, guardian of the lodge. He was memory and desire and his clay feet were famous but most of the time safely hidden behind the bar.

It was October, I remember.

There had been a frost the week before and now there was the sense of the waning year, poetic perhaps where the leaves turn red but here in the concrete merely an insinuation of passing life, a suggestion in the air of the shape of one's death. In and out of Sheridan's bar various people came and went. Even the barworld moved but all this time I did not. I sat on the bench in Lower

Three. A queen I was, under the posters that recommended the Lakes of Killarney.

"Give us a song, Carlotta!"

It was old Pat Keeley, croaking the words through his cancerous throat. I blew him a kiss and began to sing:

"The youth knelt down to tell his sins
   Nomine Dei, the youth begins
Mea Culpe he beats his breast
   And in broken murmur repeats the rest."

I sang and I sang and I sang, extracting the words from some memory vein ordinarily closed off, old ballads I had heard as a child or learned from records. *"God save Ireland, sing the heroes, God save Ireland sing they all."* Come all ye true-born Irishmen Come all ye Come all ye Comeallye Comeallye. I was as old as yonder oak. Let me sleep, let me rest, let me rest in Lower Three. You can't sleep here the sergeant says. Off wid' you now you drunkin slut and spread your washin' proper. Anna Livia Plurabelle. H C E and then I fell sideways and slipped to the floor. On the floor I remained and refused to be roused. My forehead was gashed and bleeding. My cheek was resting in the wet. Some idiot called the police. I could hear them above me, all of them. "Do you think she's dying?" someone asked. "She's never died on us yet," was the answer. Then the oxygen mask was on my face, gas rushing from the cylinder. On the stretcher my eyes opened to see the policeman who looked at me as if I were an object instead of a human being. He was a very young policeman with the *face* of a cruel baby, standing above me with his contempt, writing in his plump black book.

The ambulance was dark and seemed to sway and the alcoholic ward was filled with all the little formless fears of O'Neill. I was not quite unconscious. I felt the jab of the needle when they thrust it into my buttocks. I remember myself on my belly, one buttock pierced and punished, sobbing because the other was to go without its share of pain. Phantasies. I had them then in the alky ward, face down on the pillowless bed, praying, sobbing, pleading that someone would beat my soft ass with his fists until the flesh was bruised and the skin was black and blue. No one beat me. No one touched me, after the long sharp needle was thrust into my flesh. I slept that dreadful sleep that is filled with the fears of night and day and with the fears of heaven and hell, the drunkard's sleep that is no sleep but only a kind of waking retreat in which one seems to rise and fall, alternating life with death.

In the morning I saw the faces. All around me, those faces. It was Belsen and Buchenwald and the dungeons at Kilmainham. Soon they will take us to the gas chambers, I can remember that I thought. Soon they will come in their black tunics, bearing instruments of torture.

I did not go to the gas chamber.

When my three days were up I went to a pleasant room in Doctor's Hospital on a high floor that overlooked the park, and every morning from my window I could see the Mayor of New York get into his shiny car and drive away to his work downtown. There was Falkstein and there was the little Italian doctor with his pills and his needles to put you to sleep but with never a chopper to chop off your head. And then, my friend, there was this room, there was you, and your silent office and your fish in the front room where one taps his toes and waits until the patient who precedes him has extracted the last sixty seconds of time that he's bought.

Why that day did I stop drinking and begin working and come here? Wherefore is this day different from all other days?

I don't know, except that the monitor inside my body, inside, perhaps, my soul, had decided to call: *time! gentlemen, time!* It was me, all me. At the hospital, looking down on the mayor, the little doctor was pleased with himself and certain that he had impressed upon me the need to seek assistance. Falkstein thought he had been effective when he sat on the edge of my bed, stinking up the pretty room with the smoke from his cigar, threatening to kill the play if I did not appear for rehearsals as soon as the little doctor said I was fit to begin work. They were wrong, both of them. There had been a change in my own climate, sudden and certain as a change in the actual weather. The decision to come to this place, to sit in this chair, it was mine. I come here every day, five days in every week, and I can think of better things I might do with the thirty dollars an hour that I pay you. Yet I come. No one makes me come. There is no truant officer. Falkstein does not employ secret agents. No one follows me in the street to make himself certain I do not go to a barroom or bedroom or some private pouting room instead of coming here to this room and to you, my dear friend. Do you know that other people pay good money for the sound of my voice? As much as six dollars and sixty cents, just to hear me utter somebody else's words? But I pay you to listen to me.

Do you get my money's worth?

I come of my own free will you say? Not exactly. When I came first, last autumn, I was going through certain motions that I supposed would reassure people who for various reasons are interested in me. You know that sometimes I yearn to conform, to be a good little girl, just good, good, good, pleasing everyone all the time. Last year I was a standard figure out of a book or a play or a movie or a case history or a police blotter. I was a periodic drunkard who had just finished a period. The accepted thing is regeneration and in these days one seeks help. Being godless and well-to-do, the headshrinker's house is the place to call, rather than the priest's house. Going to a psychiatrist is the correct thing for people like myself when they are in what other people call trouble. The point is I do come. I wonder why? It is a habit, I suppose, like smoking or taking a daily walk always with the same turnings until one has memorized even the scars on the concrete pavement. One o'clock, lunch-time; Two o'clock, hairdresser; Four o'clock, French class; Five o'clock, read; Six o'clock, doctor; Seven-fifteen o'clock, dinner; Eight-fifteen o'clock, theater; Twelve o'clock, hot milk, pillow, book, and empty bed. Matinees Wednesdays and Saturdays. Sunday a free day. If I didn't come here every day, what on earth would I do with the hour between six and seven P.M.? There would be a blank space in the day. Also, you must understand it is a tax deduction and these days tax deductions are not lightly to be tossed aside.

I do not want to talk today. I shouldn't have come. I have nothing to say. I am bored. Bored with the play, bored with clothes, bored with flat ginger ale, bored with you. Most of all, bored with us, with you and me and our odd love affair. I don't suppose you would care to screw me here on the patients' couch? We could lock the door. And be very quiet. Perhaps the floor would be better. There must be a nice hard floor beneath that god-awful rug. I don't see why you object. It's my thirty dollars, and it might be good for your morale.

I make no impression on you with my free association.

You are not shocked or amused or annoyed or sexually aroused. Certainly not that. Have you ever...? Of course you have ever. After all, there are your children. Sometimes I hear them at the piano. But nowadays, I mean. Are you nothing but limp skin? Does the blood never leave your head and travel to a place between your thighs? You are a self-made eunuch, Doctor Fowler, castrated by your own brains and the idiot business with which you have stuffed them since you left the Harvard Yard.

I do not touch you. Are you laughing at me, behind your cotton curtain? After all I don't offer to get down on the floor with every tom dick and harry I meet. Nor with every harry dick and tom. I am a nice girl really and you are a very special case. Actually I am fond of you though not in that way really and I am awfully sorry for you and for your wife and for your wee wrinkly po-po that was shrunken up by Freud. I am my own woman and I am not afreud, but you live in terror that the walls will come tumbling down. Still the business should last your lifetime. Take a look at the Catholic Church. When the walls came tumbling down, up they went again and again and again and again....

Very well I will stop.

And I will apologize.

I am very rude.

O my Fowler I am heartily sorry for my sins because they offend thee who art so correct.

What am I thinking of now?

At this moment?

I am thinking of a glass of Irish whiskey on the rocks. And that is God's truth. I did not invent the answer simply to annoy you, Doctor. For the first time in all these months perhaps I have played the game strictly according to the rules. When you asked your question I was thinking of nothing else, nothing more complicated than a glass of Irish whiskey on the rocks.

What am I thinking about now? Shitshitshitshitshitshitshit shitshitshitshitshitshitshitshit.

That's what little girls are made of.

This has been a very expensive hour of silence on a not very comfortable couch. Next time I will bring my knitting.

May I move back to the chair? I don't like this position. I feel like the inmate of a brothel, waiting for a customer to be sent upstairs. Thank you. Of course I understand there is no magic in the couch itself. God knows with you in the room a girl might just as well stand or swing from the chandelier.

I have hired a firm of private detectives and asked them to look for my father. I know. You needn't ask. What am I going to do with him if the detectives find him for me? I don't know.

Nothing I suppose. I simply cannot bear it not to know where he is. Probably they will not find him. They are very reliable detectives. They did not want to take the case. They say it is one chance in a thousand.

Why do I refuse to search for him here? you ask.

Please, sir, I am a simple Irish peasant girl and you must put things to me in simple terms. The man I am looking for is Michael McBride, white, six feet two inches, ruddy complexion, two hundred odd pounds, probably alcoholic, homeless perhaps, dead perhaps. I want to tell him that he is not to blame. I am a grown woman now and I am cold as marble. When a man makes love to me he makes his love to a corpse. His manhood shrivels in the cold until it is wrinkled and absurd, a contemptible thing that humiliates instead of an object that arouses pride. Always this happens to a man if he cares for me at all. Only with those who detest me or with those others to whom I am nothing but flesh, only with these can I even pretend. I am cold, cold, cold as marble. Cold as a frozen chicken taken from the deep freeze. Sexually, I am dead. Only a necrophile would care to sleep with a thing like that. And I never thaw out. Even when I am full to the gullet with booze, booze, booze. Even then I don't thaw out. I make motions. I am an actress. I know something of anatomy. I know which parts to touch and why, when to caress like the wing of a moth and when to gouge with my polished nails or bite flesh with my white teeth. I make motions. I am an actress. But the temperature does not change. I am an ice cold sewer, a semenal sewer, a truly disposable love object.

But god damn it to hell doctor! I was not always like that. God damn the virgin mary! I was not always like that.

But that was in another country and besides the whence is dead. At sixteen years of age precisely I was an Old Testament harlot with burning limbs, breasts like honey, nipples like almonds. All that Song of Solomon crap. I was a temptress out of Nineveh, destroyer of honor, assassin of virtue. Ah god, she drives men mad! Salome where she danced. Put away the grass skirts, pop, oscar wilde has come.

Or was I simply a young girl who wanted to be screwed-screwedscrewed?

I don't know.

But I do know that I was the one who called the turns on that afternoon at the Lodge in Maine, while the blizzard blizzarded outside and we drank the French champagne. On that afternoon I was altogether without morals, without fear for myself or for anyone else. A hot box has no conscience. Who said that, Doctor? Plato? Aristotle? Karl Marx? Great men all of them, oozing truth like pus from a boil.

I remember, I remember. Standing in the bedroom that had been mine since I was an infant, stark naked in front of the mirror, holding my silk pants in my hands. I smiled at my reflection and threw the pants away. I slipped the dress over my head and pulled it down over the naked flesh of my backside. It was not a schoolgirl's dress. I was dressed like a whore, an expensive whore. My mind was a whore's mind and my soul was a whore's soul. Michael McBride, the handsome soldier, home from the wars and half drunk, used to behaving like a soldier, falling into bed where he found himself, taking anyone at all with him—he was nothing but a victim.

But he was a chosen victim, you say?

Not just someone off the street?

I agree. I see your point. Of all the men abroad on earth on that afternoon ... all of them: black men, white men, Chinese, old, young, schoolboys, collegeboys, errandboys, fat men, lean men, thin men, strong men, weak men, handsome men, ugly men ... no one else out of all those millions, equipped with the same instrument, possessed of the same desires and needs ... not one of those millions could have made me then throw my pants away and walk out across the rug with the firelight on my face, naked beneath the cloth of gold, ready to be plucked, plucked, plucked.

Yes, but I concede your point. He was a chosen victim. He was the sacrificial lamb. The word adopt. Do you know what it means? To choose for, or take to oneself, to make one's own by selection or assent. If Michael McBride adopted me then I adopted Michael McBride. I must find him, you see. It is a matter of simple justice to tell him he was not to blame. Of course I am not a fool. I do not expea that my own guilt will evaporate when I have made my declaration. You suggested—was it yesterday?— that I was determined to remain the unpunished criminal. It is an interesting idea. My life then is a fugitive's life, devoted to the evasion of justice and the avoidance of retribution. Perhaps. Someone insists that drinking is a form of self-punishment. On the other hand, someone else has said: what a lovely way to die! Perhaps it is simply my way of going into mourning for myself or for my unborn soul. Mourning they say becomes Electra. That is a fitting end to Carlotta. I shall be Elearacuted.

If I tried I could make you laugh.

But would it be worth-while? Would it be at all worthwhile? Never in my life have I seen a man with his trousers rolled. Bad form in the Ivy League. Or as Beauregard Johnson would say: don't be a bounder in the mess, old boy.

Why do I do the things I do? Why did I drink at Sheridan's instead of at Sardi's or at Twenty-One? Why did I drink in a place that is encrusted with failure, surrounded by abandoned hope, instead of in one of the bright places where the air is charged with success, as if the odor of success were sprayed into the air from a gun, the way they spray small-town movie houses with that awful perfume? Was I seeking a preview of my future? Oh no my friend. I am much too selfish. I told you that at Sheridan's snug I was a member of the lodge. It was a lie. I was only a visitor, an outsider, holding a temporary permit.

I am uncommitted.

What is the fashionable word? *Engagé? Engagée?*

That is what I am not.

As an alcoholic, as a woman, as an actress, as sinner, as saint...I am uncommitted. I am not engaged. My mind is accurate enough and I read many books. I am not a member of the Second Sex or the First or the Third. Sportive, n'est-ce pas? I am like an intricate modern machine, a complex of tubes and transistors designed to perform miracles that no one wants to have performed. I am an intricate beautiful machine, but I do not work. I am out of order. Kaput. Not yet in operation. Why? The repairmen are very stupid and I do mean you. It will not help to overhaul me, change a fuse, add a tube, tighten a wire, kick me with a frustrated foot in the hope that anger will put me in motion. It is a matter of power supply. I have simply not been plugged in. Here you are, a trained psychoanalyst, complete with office, tape recorders, waiting room with tropical fish, signed diplomas on the walls, and yet you waste your time and mine. Look behind the machine, Doctor, along the baseboard. Find the cord and plug it in. You will be surprised, I promise you that. The picture will be strong and clear, no trace of a ghost at all, and the sound will be strictly Hi-Fi. But that would be too simple, wouldn't it, Dr. Fowler? If you insist on asking a complicated question you will get a complicated answer. Let us go back to the more elementary questions.

Bed-wetting? To be sure.

Thumb-sucking? Guilty but punished.

Temper tantrums? Oh yes.

Masturbation? Ah, we come to a thornier problem. The answer is no. At least not successfully.

Should I begin now, do you think, to fill the gap in my childhood experience? Don't tell me to shut up. I will say what I please. It's my money and my time. If you don't like what comes out of my mouth go and sit in the waiting room and look at your damned fish until my boughten hour is up.

I am sorry.

I talk nonsense.

But I have a feeling we are getting nowhere.

I do not think that you can help me or that I can help myself here. I should be moving and on my way, looking for myself in the bright sunlight, not here in this quiet room.

CHAPTER FIVE

PARIS IS FULL OF PRIESTS, MAVOURNEEN

ARLOTTA woke up slowly to an unfamiliar room. Above her was a crystal chandelier, set into an elaborately ornamented plaster escutcheon. The walls were papered with faded cabbage roses. The windows were like tall doors, covered with net curtains the color of dirty underwear, through which grey indeterminate light entered the room. Is it morning she wondered, or evening? The corners of the room were in shadow. Against the wall was a lop-sided armoire, one door hanging open. From the street rose the sound of a horse on cobbles, then the roar of a motorbike, the engine frantically gunned. The air was close and smelled of carpeting and dusty plush. After a little Carlotta became aware that someone slept in the other bed. For some time she lay on her back, contemplating the chandelier, disinclined to look at her companion. Then she raised herself in the bed and turned her head. A girl slept peacefully, dark hair strewn on the soggy pillow. She was young and probably attractive in the unwashed, bohemian manner. Carlotta did not recognize her nor did she recognize the room, which, it now became apparent, was a bedroom in a third-class French hotel.

On a chair were the clothes she had worn the day before, suit neatly folded, shoes placed carefully beside the chair. I never undressed myself last night, she thought, trying to remember where she had been, what she had done, which people she had been with during the hours before she had been brought here to this room. She recalled getting dressed in her room at the hotel, after a long perfumed bath. She remembered having drinks in the bar downstairs and vaguely she remembered a tall German with a sabre scar who had been so persistent she had left the hotel and gone somewhere else, but where she had gone she could not remember. Again she looked at the sleeping girl. What happened last night? I wonder. Did I make love to Miss Cruddydrawers? Did she make love to me? Or did we entertain Japanese sailors until some improbable hour?

She got out of bed and went to the window. She was wearing her slip, wrinkled from sleep. The old carpet felt like a stiff brush against the soles of her feet. She pulled back the net curtain and looked down into the street. There was a cobbled square with a fountain that once had been a well, surrounded by benches occupied by old men in berets, noses buried in newspapers. There was sunlight and poetic morning haze. Beyond the square was an old church, grey-black with centuries of soot, making a color scheme like that in her fashionable French paintings. On the corner was a café with a bright-colored awning that said: *Slavia—Bière des Gourmets.* There was a sense of mid-morning. Carlotta frowned, looking at the empty tables in front of the café. The square was unfamiliar. She had no idea of her whereabouts or of how she came to be here instead of safe in her own hotel.

She let the curtain fall back into place and turned to look at the sleeping girl. I never pick up girls, she thought. Men sometimes by accident, but never girls. I do not like it. It disgusts me. That is an established fact of my life. Still, this is Paris. It is spring. And apparently I was the one who was picked up. The girl slept on. She is quite pretty, Carlotta decided. Lush type. Ruth. Probably Jewish. And quite clean really. I should not have called her Miss Cruddydrawers, even to myself. Perhaps I am entering a Lesbian phase, now that my thirties are in sight. God forbid! she said to herself. It must be worse than drinking. She had known them in Hollywood—the insatiable, predatory dykes, with their stupid mercenary little girls and their retinues of pansies.

In a corner of the room was a washstand bolted to the wall. On the floor beside it was a bidet, the porcelain crazed and badly chipped. Carlotta sloshed her face with water and dried herself on a thin huck towel

"Good morning!"

She heard the voice behind her and turned. The girl sat up in bed, long hair falling over her shoulders and breasts.

"Good morning," said Carlotta. "Or is it afternoon? I can't seem to find my watch."

"It's locked in the drawer with your money and the rest of your jewelry," the girl said. "In this hotel it is sound practice to lock up anything that's worth more than a hundred francs."

The voice was American, mid-western or western New York, Carlotta guessed, though part of the accent had been lost in transit.

"How do you feel?" the girl asked.

Carlotta shrugged and said she felt as well as she had any right to feel. She sat down on a straight-backed chair that had a deformed cane seat. The cane bit into the flesh of her behind through the thin silk of her slip. She welcomed the sharp pain. Any minor pain was good during the first phase of a hangover.

"Look here," she said firmly. "I don't make a habit of drawing blanks, but last night must have been an exception. I have no idea of where I am or of who you are or of why I'm here."

"You're in Montparnasse," the girl said. "If you listen you can hear the sound of the trains sometimes. We are right behind the station. This is my room, such as it is. My name is Betty Miller. I brought you home with me last night." She looked curiously at Carlotta, then said, "You mean you really don't remember anything?"

Carlotta shook her head.

"You don't remember the place in St. Germain des Prés where you took off all your clothes and danced?"

Carlotta frowned intently. "That is out of character for me," she said.

"Maybe," said Betty Miller. "Anyway, it wasn't much of a dance and getting you dressed was one hell of a job."

"Why did you bother?" Carlotta asked. "Why did you bring me here?"

"You had to be dressed," Betty Miller said. "Even in Paris it is against the law to walk the streets without any clothes. As for bringing you here, well, you had to sleep somewhere. In the cellar club where you passed out sleeping is not permitted. Of the various types who seemed eager to take you home with them, I thought I was the most harmless."

Carlotta rubbed her temples and tried to remember; she could not.

"You didn't seem to remember where you were staying in Paris," Betty Miller went on. "When we asked you the name of your hotel all you would give was an address on East Sixty-seventh Street in New York. I am a pal to all drunks but the cab fare to East Sixty-seventh Street is a little high for my pocketbook."

"East Sixty-seventh Street," said Carlotta. "Why did I want to go there, I wonder?"

She remembered the other day, standing in front of her mother's house, seeing her mother through the window. All at once in a rush of memory the smell of the place invaded her senses and she covered her face with her hands, feeling ill and almost frightened. After a moment it passed. "I suppose I should thank you," she said to her companion. "As a matter of fact, I do thank you."

"That's all right," said Betty Miller. "Take me home with you sometime. By the looks of your clothes, your pad should be better than this one." She hesitated, then said, "The only thing is, I'm sorry we didn't find Mike McBride."

"What?" said Carlotta. She felt her stomach muscles tighten. There was a rush of blood to her head. How much did I talk? she asked herself. What did I say and to whom?

"The guy you were looking for last night," Betty Miller explained.

"Do you know him?" asked Carlotta.

"Who doesn't?" was the answer. "Around St. Germain des Prés, I mean. Finding him though, that's another thing. Especially if his check from the States has just arrived and he owes you money. You never find him then."

"Check from the States?" Carlotta said.

"He gets a check every month," said Betty Miller. "By the last of the month he's always broke and borrowing."

"Does he owe you money?" Carlotta asked. She had some vague idea of paying his debt, if there was a debt.

"Not me," her companion said. "Mike doesn't borrow from the poor, I'll say that for him. He's a drunk but he is a gentleman."

Motionless Carlotta sat, the chair seat hurting her flesh, torn between an impulse to take this girl by the throat and pry from her whatever she knew and an inclination to run from the truth, whatever the truth might be.

"You sure wanted to find him last night," Betty Miller said. "We must have been in twenty dives, places Mike goes to. And you must have spent a fortune in money, in case you think I robbed your purse, when you get to look."

"It doesn't matter," said Carlotta.

"Sure it matters," said Betty Miller. "I'm a free loader but I'm not a thief." She got out of bed naked and rubbed the skin of her thighs briskly. "God! Coffee!" she said. There was an old-fashioned telephone attached to the wall between the beds. After a good deal of jiggling, breakfast was ordered. It came with surprising speed, a tray holding coffee, hot milk, two soggy crescent rolls, borne by a very old waiter who seemed unperturbed by

Betty Miller's nakedness. He put down the tray and said, "Service, Madame," and departed. Betty Miller poured the coffee.

"Are you an old girl of Mike's, from the States?" she asked.

"You might put it that way," said Carlotta.

"I wonder who sends him the money," Betty Miller said musingly, biting into a croissant. "Some people say it's his daughter. You know, the actress, Carlotta McBride. At least he swears she's his daughter but with Mike you never know what to believe and what to skip."

"I wouldn't know about the money," said Carlotta. She had the feeling that it was disloyal to sit here talking about him with someone who knew nothing of his past.

She finished her coffee then dressed herself and looked around for her purse. Betty Miller got out of her chair, searched for a key under the rug, and unlocked the drawer of the armoire. "The family safe," she explained, giving Carlotta her handbag, watch, gold necklace, earrings.

Carlotta put on some lipsick, thinking, as she looked at the mirror, that for a girl who had passed out she was doing very well indeed. She wanted a drink but not desperately. There was a dull ache in her temples but her eyes were clear.

"If you really want to find Mike, the thing to do is to go to the Bar Montana and wait 'til he shows up," said Betty Miller thoughtfully. "You may wait two, three nights, maybe even a week, but sooner or later he'll show up there. If he doesn't show by eight o'clock though, you might as well take off. It's his early place."

"The Bar Montana?" Carlotta said.

"It is a Bar Américain, across from the Church of St. Germain des Prés. I don't go there myself because it's too expensive and I don't care for the people, but Mike likes it. You'll find him there, sooner or later, if you don't find somebody else first."

"Thank you," Carlotta said. She opened her purse. There was a wad of money, stuffed into the change purse. She looked at Betty Miller and said, "Can I...?"

"I'm broke," said Betty Miller. "I'll take a thousand francs if you can spare it."

Carlotta offered her five thousand.

"I said mille francs," the girl objected. "What do you think I am, some kind of a whore?"

Carlotta put the five away and gave the girl a thousand francs. She hesitated, then said, "What do you do? Here in Paris, I mean?"

Betty Miller shrugged her shoulders and looked around her at the shabby room. "What does anybody do?" she asked. "Just live, I guess. After a fashion."

They shook hands. Carlotta went down a steep and carpeted flight of stairs, past the hall porter's cage, into the little square. She walked until she came to a café. She had not wanted to sit in the one under Betty Miller's window. She ordered black coffee and an amer picon and sat in the pleasant northern sunlight. The morning haze was gone now and the day was fair. People passed to and fro in the Carrefour Montparnasse. When she had finished the drink, Carlotta relaxed. She felt the tides of Paris around her, the subtle rhythms. How long have I been here? she wondered, trying to count back, losing track of the days. A boy passed, wearing a cap that said *France Soir*. Carlotta bought a paper and consulted the date-line. It was Saturday. She had been in Paris for three days.

Establishing the time scheme made her feel less disoriented. The first day she remembered clearly. She had bathed and changed clothes after the drive into Paris from Orly, then gone at once to the address given her in the detective agency's letter. The house was an old mansion in the faubourg St. Germain that had been converted into expensive flats. Behind a wicket sat the concierge, brooding over a newspaper, an old man with one arm, faded medal ribbons pinned to his soggy lapel. He shook his head. "Monsieur McBride? He has not been here since a year, Madame." "But that's impossible," she had protested. The old man had shrugged. "Perhaps it is six months," he said. "In any case, Madame, for a certainty he is here no longer. The apartment he occupied is now let to a Danish lady of great distinction." "But where will I find him?" she had asked. "Who knows?" the old man said. "Perhaps in Paris, perhaps in Ireland, Madame. God knows he talked about Ireland when he had taken too much to drink." "But you must have a forwarding address," she had said desperately. "None, Madame," the concierge told her. "But his mail?" she had said. "His mail did not come here, Madame," the old man said. "He is not the usual man, you must understand, this Monsieur McBride."

She had given the old man some money and walked up the narrow street. At the prefecture the police were charming but regretful. Such information was to be given out only on authority from a higher quarter. The request must be put in writing and passed through the proper sequence of officials. Of necessity, this took time. One must understand that in France the individual's right to privacy was a sacred thing, for the protection of which much blood had been shed. It was not a matter with which the police were permitted to tamper. Perhaps in America these things are ordered differently. However, madame was in France....

What did I do after that? Carlotta asked herself, sitting on the terrace of the Café Rotônde with Saturday's paper on her lap, a third amer picon at her elbow. She remembered being in the Ritz Bar and later on in Harry's, where she had pasted money to the mirror and eaten a dozen vile hot dogs, meat tasting like embalmed flesh. There had been people at Harry's, writers and reporters, she remembered. There had been steak in a restaurant somewhere near the abbatoirs. She remembered a long taxi ride on the Avenue Jean Jaurès. She remembered the beef on her plate, wedge-shaped and succulent.

Desperately as a quiz contestant trying for two hundred thousand dollars, she prodded the corners of her mind, trying to remember the name of the restaurant, the faces of the people she had been with. It was no use. There was vague recollection of her hotel room that overlooked the Place Vendôme, and she dredged up disconnected episodes, flashes of various bars and various faces. She could not remember her meeting with the girl Betty Miller nor could she recover a picture of the existentialist cellar in which she had disrobed and danced for the patrons. She sipped the astringent drink. I must be careful, she told herself. I must not black out again.

She rode to the Place Vendôme in a taxi, collected her key and went upstairs. The hall porter was impassive. His disinterest made her more embarrassed than if he had leered suggestively and made some reference to her absence for the night.

In her room she went at once to the little desk and wrote the WORD MONTANA on a scrap of hotel stationery, not trusting herself to remember the name. She paused, then wrote beneath it: 5:30-8:30.

Then she took off her clothes and lay down on the big bed. On the glass-topped chest of drawers stood a bottle of Irish whiskey, almost full. When did I buy that? she wondered. The room was peaceful, a big luxurious chamber with comfortable chairs and a thick rug and the smell of wealth. Beneath her body the bed was soft, the pillow case smooth to her cheek. She closed her eyes and rested, held safe in the rich quiet room. She enjoyed luxury. All her life she had been used to it. What must it be like to live as does that girl, Betty Miller, she wondered, in a shabby Left Bank room that must be intolerably cold in winter, without money, without clothes, probably hungry part of the time, always obliged to cadge drinks. Would I enjoy drinking if I didn't have plenty of money? She could not imagine herself living the way Betty Miller lived or the way the women in Sheridan's existed, sitting patiently at the bar waiting for someone to buy them a drink out of alcoholic pity or contempt or in return for conversation. To drink in the gutter or on the edge of the gutter—it was a prospect that held no appeal. When Carlotta was drinking she enjoyed the actual physical spending of money and in a bar she enjoyed being the Lady Bountiful who was always good for a drink or a touch. She knew women with plenty of money who hated to spend it on themselves, women who seemed to take a kind of cannibalistic pleasure in obliging men to buy things for them, especially if the men could not afford it.

I am not like that, she thought.

She disliked gifts and almost never used the things that people gave her. What were the words she had read in a book? Unable to love or inspire love. The words had struck her like a series of blows. They were written for me, those words, she had thought. I am unloved. I do not love. Least of all do I love myself.

Yet he loved me, her mind objected. He must have loved me. And I loved him. I have always loved him or at least I cannot love anyone else. I cannot bear it to be touched by anyone else in this world or the next. It makes me vomit to be touched unless I am drunk, drunk, drunk, and then of course I am dead in my body.

"Montana," she said, half aloud. "Bar Américain, across from the church of St. Germain des Prés." It doesn't matter. It is written down. She closed her eyes and permitted herself to drift into half sleep but she was never unaware of the porcelain clock on the marble mantelpiece. The clock had an elegant, feminine tick; from time to time while she rested Carlotta consulted its gilt face. At four o'clock she got up and took a warm bath, then clothed herself with great care, putting on a black silk dress that revealed a considerable amount of shoulder and a pair of suave black suede shoes, cut and sewn by a Florentine artist.

The nap had refreshed her and the warm bath calmed her nerves and eased the tension in her muscles. I feel good! she said to herself. The bottle of Irish whiskey stood on the chest of drawers untouched. It is extraordinary, thought Carlotta. I have no real desire for a drink. It must be that I am a false alcoholic. A real addict could not resist the bottle there in full view, bought and paid for, especially with no one to watch him, to disapprove, to stop his hand.

The lobby of the hotel was like a movie set, bright with well-dressed people talking in fashionable accents in half a dozen languages—Riviera riffraff, men in the sleek Italian mode, fitted jackets, effeminate shoes, women with real jewels, contessas and principessas and duchesas in their Roman clothes, almost obscenely smart, exuding costly perfume and sinister self-confidence, the well-bred, contemptuous vanquished. Carlotta paused while they flowed around her. What would they think, these people, if I told them I now am going out into the mild French evening to look for my father who is not my father but only my lover of long ago? They would think nothing, she decided. They would be neither shocked nor amused, these predestined survivors. They would be bored. They would murmur, "How interesting," and gracefully pass on to the place where champagne was being poured. She despised and envied them. Meaninglessly, she feared them. They were sure of themselves as she was not.

"I am Carlotta McBride."

She had said it a thousand times, a thousand thousand. The words had no power to convince her. She might as well have said, "I am the moon," or "I am the rock on yonder shore," or "I am the Power and the Glory."

She stepped out into the Place Vendôme. The elegant stone was touched with pink. The tiny smart shops glistened. The column that Courbet once pulled down threw an umbrous phallus across the brush swept cobbles. It was the center of all elegance, hearthstone of the world of women. She could not call up a picture of Courbet and his Communards filling the square with the sound of their clogs, spitting on the well-swept stone, singing as they pulled the column down.

The doorman saluted and held the door; Carlotta stepped into a taxi. "Bar Montana if you please, in St. Germain des Prés," she said. "With quickness, Madame," the driver responded. The cab moved into the meshing traffic in the Place de la Concorde. In the fragrant evening light the beauty was like the beauty of music. How does it escape the cliché, like the other things one has seen forever in photographs, films and reproductions? Carlotta asked herself. The sunrise can become a cliché but not the Place de la Concorde. She tasted the thrill of Paris, crossing the river on a narrow bridge. I must be alive, she told herself. I am touched, I am moved, I am humbled, just as is everyone else.

The Bar Montana was like a place to be found in New York in the east Fifties: a narrow underlighted room with dark mirrors and chromium and highly polished mahogany. Only the caissière on her high stool suggested that the place was French. At one end of the bar was a collaboration of homosexuals—quite bizarre, with earrings and bracelets and bleached hair. In the back of the room were miniscule tables occupied by girls in black jerseys and blue jeans, wearing lank pony tails, faces bare of make-up but completely powdered, lips and all, so the faces seemed to have been drained of blood. Are they props? Carlotta wondered. Characters out of an existentialist novel written for the American market.

There were no Americans. The existentialist girls were French. The homosexuals were mostly French and English, with a pair of Danes and a dark youth who looked Greek or Lebanese. Carlotta sat on a high stool and considered the arrangement of bottles displayed behind the bar. There was John Jameson and she ordered that. It was eight hundred francs, a shocking price, and scotch she knew was nearly as much yet scotch was what everyone else was drinking, even the moody blue-jeaned girls, little Lesbian prostitutes who sat in the morbid violet light waiting for what might come along.

Carlotta waited too, silent as the little perverted whores, drinking slowly, for a time aware of the twittering pederasts, then aware of nothing but the clock on the wall. At eight o'clock she began to look at the watch on her wrist. "If he's not there by eight he won't come," Betty Miller had warned her. She decided to wait a little longer. At eight fifteen he came into the bar. She recognized his silhouette at once as he stood in the doorway for a moment, three steps above floor level. He came down into the bar. Carlotta turned away. His hair was white. He carried a blackthorn stick and walked with a considerable limp. He had lost some weight and his eyes were like the haunted eyes of a tortured priest who has been obliged to confess to a structure of falsehood. The serving girl at the bar greeted him with a short handshake, French fashion. "Whiskey, if you please," he said in English. "Irish whiskey."

"Instantly, Monsieur McBride."

Carlotta forced herself to turn slowly on her stool. He was facing her, glass in hand, one elbow on the bar. For an instant their eyes met. He did not recognize her. Then he tossed off the drink and touched his mouth with the back of his hand. He is quite drunk, Carlotta said to herself. He has been drinking for days, perhaps for weeks. He has lost the sense of time, perhaps even the sense of place.

"Good evening," she said, looking directly at him.

"Good evening to you," he said.

"We are both drinking Jameson, I see," she said. "Will you have one with me?"

"I won't refuse you," he said.

They had a drink, then another. Carlotta touched his hand. "You don't recognize me," she said.

He looked at her and frowned. "You have the advantage of me," he admitted.

"I am Carlotta," she said. "I am Carlotta McBride."

He stared at her then shook his head. "Carlotta McBride is a pale blonde with hair the color of wheat in the sun."

"Look at me," Carlotta commanded. "Look at my eyes, my mouth. Forget my hair."

He shook his head. "Wouldn't I know my own daughter?" he said logically. "But you must have a drink with me."

"No," she said, opening her purse.

He shrugged his shoulders and permitted her to pay. It is not the moment of protest, Carlotta understood. Later, when he is much drunker or later still when he is sober, it will be possible to reach his mind, but not now, not at this moment.

They sat in the dark and corrupt bar, drinking Irish whiskey, hardly speaking, close together. "Will you have dinner with me?" Carlotta asked. "I am a stranger in Paris and alone."

"I'm an old man and a drunkard," he said. "Paris is full of young blood. You might even find someone who'd buy your dinner for you."

"Please," she said.

"If you like," he said. "It would be an act of kindness at that. Left to myself I'd stand here until it was too late to get a proper meal at all."

They went out into the night, passing the terraces of famous cafés, people at tables pushed close together, an endemic cloud above them of cerebral conversation, so that a man with a quick hand might have snatched excellent phrases out of the highly charged spring air. It was a vivid, clear night and the boulevard was crowded. Facing them as they left the bar was the ancient tower of St. Germain des Prés, serene against the April sky, permanent as the clear moon itself.

"We'll go to the Italian's," he decided, taking her arm and guiding her across the wide and hazardous street. "He always gives you a good feed and it's not too dear."

"Wherever you like," Carlotta said.

He released her arm when they reached the curb, walking beside her, using his stick. "Only a fool would manage to get wounded twice in the same leg, now wouldn't he?" he asked cheerfully.

Carlotta stopped in the street and closed her eyes for a moment. She could remember the scar on his leg as he stood naked in the winter light, a mind picture clear and unreal as an expert photograph in color.

"Is anything wrong?" he asked, touching her arm.

"No. Nothing," she said.

They went on, leaving the lighted street. The restaurant was on the second floor of an old house in a narrow alley, a long room jammed with people, menu chalked on a blackboard, sawdust on the floor, waiters who looked like Sicilian banditti. The proprietor was plump and efficient and wore the rosette of the Legion of Honor.

The food was good. Carlotta ate deliberately, handling her knife and fork as if they were dissecting tools. She was frightened. It was not until they were halfway through the meal that he looked at her steadily and said, "You are Carlotta. You have dyed your hair."

"Yes," she said, putting down her knife and fork. "I am Carlotta."

For several seconds neither of them spoke. Carlotta's heart was pounding. He knew me in spite of my hair, she thought. He must have known me, back there in the bar. He is afraid as I am afraid. He sat back in his chair, looking steadily at her now.

"I thought sometimes that you would come," he said. "And sometimes, when I was very drunk, I thought that I would go to you. But it never seemed a good idea in the morning, you understand."

"I know about that," she said.

He looked at the food on his plate as if, suddenly, it disgusted him, then pushed the plate away. "I can't eat," he said. He raised his head and looked for a waiter. "Monsieur McBride?" "Bring me my bottle," he said. Almost at once the waiter brought a half-filled bottle of Irish whiskey. He poured a drink into Carlotta's wine glass, then filled his own. "They don't serve liquor here," he explained. "Only wine. So I keep a bottle in the kitchen for such eventualities."

Carlotta touched the bottle with the tips of her fingers. She was at the border of danger and she felt it. With a kind of drunkard's clairvoyance, she understood that she could sit here with him and finish this bottle, go out with him and buy another, and continue drinking, the two of them, until one or the other fell unconscious or dead. Or she could draw back now, refuse the sign, refuse to cross the border. He drank his whiskey at a gulp. Hers was untouched.

"You're not drinking?" he said.

"I'll finish my dinner," she said.

Very carefully, she began to eat. He poured himself another drink. "Why did you come?" he asked. "What are you doing here in Paris?"

"I came to see you," she said.

"But why?" he said. "You must have known what you'd find."

"Why did I come?" she asked. "I don't know. I thought I knew, but I was mistaken. I wanted forgiveness, you see."

He leaned forward and touched her wrist. For the first time there was in him the spark of warmth that had once been there. "Ah, mavourneen," he said. "Paris is full of priests. Why do you come to me for something I haven't got to give?"

"No priest can help me," she said. "I do not believe in God. Where else would I come to be forgiven?"

"You don't look to the past for forgiveness," he said. "You look for that in the future, if you have one."

He was drinking steadily from the bottle and his voice was thick. Carlotta finished her dinner and asked for the bill. As she counted out the money he said, "I'd pay if I could, you understand. It's just that at this moment I'm short."

"It doesn't matter," she said.

In the street he staggered a little. The steel tip of his cane punctuated his injured gait. They went downhill, through the dark alley, and came out into the light.

"Where shall we go?" she asked.

"We can go to my place if you like," he said. "It's not far from here. But first, if you don't mind, we should stop for a bottle at the Montana."

She gave him money from her purse and they went into the Montana. The bar was very crowded now, filled with diseased sexuality. "Why do you come here?" she asked, while they waited to be served.

"Why not?" he said. "Here, you see, I can get drunk and feel superior to the people around me."

Of course, she thought. I am the same way at Sheridan's.

"Also, it makes me homesick," he said, wedging his way to the bar.

When he had the bottle, they went out into the night again and walked to the place where he lived, a small hotel on a back street, the entrance guarded by an old woman who sat stoically behind her grilled window. There was an ancient elevator, self-service, operated by means of a rope. His room was like Betty Miller's room, but smaller and even more shabby. There were two electric lights of improbably low wattage, bringing into the room a suggestion of death. There were the same curtains, made of stuff like dirty underwear, and the same faded wall-paper, the same cracked bidet, the same sagging wardrobe.

"A bit different from East Sixty-seventh," he said, at once beginning to open the bottle. "I had a better place for a while, but it seemed a waste of money." With some effort, he pulled the cork and sighed with relief. "Sit down and I'll pour you a drink," he said.

There was a stiffbacked wing chair covered with spotted tapestry. Carlotta sat down. He poured drinks into heavy glasses and handed one to her.

"*Slainte,*" he said, tossing it off.

Carlotta sipped the whiskey. What was it the old Irish actor had told her? One an hour, no more no less, and you won't be drunk until the day is over. It is a false scheme, she thought, like all the schemes evolved by drunks. In the end, if you drink at all, drunk is what you get.

He took the other chair, the bottle on the floor beside him. The night was silent. Then there was a sudden, illegal horn blast from the street. He sat up as though someone had stabbed him.

"Jesus, Mary and Joseph!" he said.

Carlotta sipped her whiskey again. She was drunk, she understood. She must be drunk. But she was ice cold drunk and her mind was clear. She looked around the dreary room, then looked at him. He was staring at the glass in his hand, as if he expected the whiskey to give him the words he wanted to speak. Then he sighed again. It was like the sigh of an old woman who weeps outside the prison wall, a sound that was filled with formal grief, expressing hopelessness. Carlotta shuddered; almost it was like being in the presence of death, or at the side of someone about to die.

"Paris is full of priests," he said, repeating himself. "Why do you come to me, mavourneen?"

"You loved me once," she said.

"But that was in another country…"

He sat up straight in the chair and shook his head violently, as if he tried to shake himself out of the alcoholic swamp. Then he looked at Carlotta.

"I loved you once," he said. "I think maybe I love you still, as much as there's any love in me. But what happened to us that day in Maine, and the other days, with the snow outside and the fire going and the wine and whiskey flowing—what happened to us then, that had nothing to do with love. It was an incident, Carlotta. Something that happened. Like murder or birth or maybe like a death in battle. It had no beginning and no end. It was something that happened."

"You ran away," she said.

He nodded. "Yes," he said. "I ran away. And so did you, I take it. But I have stopped running. I am beyond running. I have surrendered and this is my home. But you, you are still on the run. I am sorry for you, Carlotta. I pity you. It is a terrible thing to run, to stumble and fall, to pick yourself up, and to go on running, blind and exhausted."

"So you know?" she said.

"Oh yes, I know," he said. "I ran for a time, you see. And then I came here, because I wanted to change my life. It was an idea I got from a book. It didn't work. I came here to change my life, but I haven't changed it. I've only stopped it, after a fashion."

Carlotta finished the whiskey in her glass. I could stay here with him, she thought. They would send me money from New York. I could stay here with him and drink. We could find a better place than this. One of those little apartments, maybe, on the Ile St. Louis. We could drink all the time, he and I, until we died, or until one of us died or one of us went mad. She put her glass on the floor, got up and crossed to where he sat, kneeling beside his chair. She took his hand. "You loved me once," she said.

He kissed her cheek. They embraced and for a moment clung together. Then he drew back. "No, Carlotta," he said. "Don't make a fool of me again, girl."

She got up, humiliated, and went back to her chair. He drank from the bottle then offered it to her. She shook her head. He wiped his mouth with the back of his hand. "I disgust you," he said. "I am an old man and a drunkard, a disgusting old man."

But I am young, Carlotta thought. How long must I go on as I am, killing myself every day, whether I drink or not?

"I loved your mother once," he said suddenly, as if he had been struck with an idea.

"She is not my mother," said Carlotta sharply.

He leaned forward, peering at her, the whiskey bottle in his hands. "She is your mother all right," he said. "I am not your father, but she is your mother."

"I don't believe you," Carlotta said.

He ignored her, staring at the bottle, fascinated by the words that were printed on the label. "I loved your mother once," he said. "When she was young and handsome, alive, you see, a human being. She never loved me." His voice was thick with the whiskey and his words came slowly. Stiffly, Carlotta sat in her chair and listened. It was like listening to a forced confession, extracted by means of torture or drugs.

"She hated me. She hated me twice. Once when we married and later on, when she found that I couldn't make children for her. It was your father she loved and then hated, I suppose, in the way she hates all men, except maybe the infant Jesus, and I'm not sure sometimes she doesn't hate him worse than any of the men on earth."

He raised his head to look at Carlotta, then drank from his bottle.

"She loved your father all right though. She loved him enough to let him get into her breeches, though they weren't married. I knew him, you understand. He was a lad named Jimmy Vincent and a wild boy he was too. Oh, he would have married her all right. He was wild but he was loaded with Irish honor. The trouble was he got himself drunk on Irish whiskey and killed himself in a bright red car he liked to drive over the Long Island roads at seventy-eighty miles an hour. He didn't mean to kill himself. It's just that a man isn't much of a driver with a quart of this inside of him."

He lifted the bottle to the light, looked at it, then drank again. He was very drunk, but it was impossible to doubt that what he said was the truth. Carlotta sat motionless, as if she had been paralyzed. Here were answers to questions that she had been asking for almost a third of her life, yet they did not make the effect she might have expected.

"I was a young lad then, working for your grandfather Costain," he went on. "I loved your mother and the old man knew it. She had you inside of her belly and young Jimmy Vincent was dead. I was Irish and I was Catholic and I had been to Harvard College. The old man put it to me straight. 'She won't refuse you, Michael,' he said. 'You have my word for that, lad.' And she did not refuse me. She obeyed her father. She married me in St. Patrick's Cathedral, in front of a bishop, with the sin inside of her body, and she hated me from that instant, as much as if I'd killed young Jimmy Vincent with my own two hands."

Carlotta began to cry now.

"Don't cry for me, Carlotta," he said. He drank from the bottle and gagged. With difficulty, he got up and went to the sink on the wall, ran a glass of water and drank it. "I am not worth crying about," he said, without pride or anger or melodramatics. "I told you I stopped running, and it is true. But when I stopped I had left behind me, somehow, whatever manner of man I had been."

She looked at him. He sagged in the chair. She had come a long distance, in masquerade, to help or to be helped and to be set free. There was no help to be received or given, yet she thought that somehow she had glimpsed her freedom, far off and in the dark.

"You will stay here then?" she asked.

"Yes, I shall stay here," he said, looking around his room, the impoverished yellow light on his face. "The army sends me a few dollars to make up for my bad leg. I have a few dollars of my own. I am warm here. I don't hurt a living soul, even, any longer, myself. So I shall stay here and die, but not, I'm afraid, for a long time."

Carlotta got up and went to the window, pulling back the curtains. The street was dark. Far off there was a smudge of light from the boulevard. She dropped the curtain and turned back into the room. There was the morgue-like sense of death now more intense than before.

"And you, Carlotta," he said. "What about you?"

"I am still running," she said. "I would like to stop. But not here. Not like this."

He drank again and lifted himself to his feet, moving toward her across the shabby rug. "Ah, mavourneen," he said. "Stay and finish the bottle with me." He tried to embrace her and lurched badly, almost falling to the floor. Then he sat down heavily. His head fell forward. He will sleep in the chair, Carlotta thought. He will never get into his bed now. She knelt beside him and methodically began to undress him, unlacing his shoes, pulling them off, then pulling off his socks and his trousers. She had trouble with the knot of his tie and almost broke a fingernail. At last he was naked, and on his feet, swaying, almost unconscious. She opened the wardrobe and searched for his pajamas. There were none.

"Sleep raw," he mumbled. "Always sleep raw."

She looked at his body, forcing her eyes to focus on the twin wounds that marked his leg. Twenty millimetre, he had said. That was what had made the first one. What made the other? she wondered. The flesh was withered and looked as if it had been clawed by a large wild animal, but the scars were old now and healed. She remembered a phrase that Doctor Fowler once had used: "The best we can hope for, you understand, is a good scar. A good clean scar."

"Come, Michael, get into your bed," she said, taking his arm, leading him to the soggy bed.

"Stay and finish the bottle," he pleaded, as if it were the only idea left in his mind.

"No," she said.

"Put it near the bed then," he begged. "Put it here on the table."

He got into the bed and she covered him. Then she put the bottle and the tooth glass on his night table. She opened her purse and took out most of what money she had, putting the big limp notes under the bottle.

"Good night, Michael," she said.

He was already unconscious. She bent to kiss his cheek.

"Goodbye, Michael," she said.

She switched off the miserly lights and went out of the room. Unwilling to wait for the elevator she went down the narrow stairs. She stepped into the dark street and walked downhill toward the Boulevard St. Germain, ignoring the heavy traffic, causing brakes to shriek in anguish, prompting an hysterical chorus of horns. A boy on a motor scooter nearly killed her. He came to a stop, burning his tires. He was a tall dark boy with rich auburn hair, wearing a dark blue sweater with a turtle neck. "Is it that you do not want to go on living, Madame?" he said gravely, staring at her.

"Oh, yes. I want to live," she said.

She went on across the street. There was a little park. Above her loomed the gothic stones of St. Germain des Prés. The night was warm but Carlotta shuddered as if from the cold. She went through a tiny side door, made her duty to the altar, and knelt in a pew at the back of the church. The golden fires of the altar blazed, shot with the flames of a thousand candles. Old women prayed in batches. The images of God and of God's friends were high on the tall aristocratic walls. For a long time Carlotta remained on her knees, hypnotized by the altar lights, not moving except to breathe.

"I wish that I believed," she said to herself at last. "In You or in the devil or even in my simple self."

She thought of the man that she had loved, naked and drunk in his dirty room, whiskey and money on the table beside him. I will send him money from time to time, a little, she thought, toward the end of the month, when he will need it. I have nothing else to send him.

Why did I come? she asked herself, kneeling in the ancient church, yearning for truth as she never had sought it in Doctor Fowler's office. Was it to see him as he is now, degraded, helpless, reduced to a kind of inferential begging, castrated, if one wants to use their ghastly terminology? What was it that I wanted? To drink with him? To sleep with him again, perhaps? To kill him with words or with a sharp knife? Or was it simply that I was moved to return to the scene of the crime?

Two old women passing out of the church stared at her. Carlotta realized that she was crying, her face raised to the altar lights. She dried her cheeks with a handkerchief and rose to her feet. Her knees were stiff. She hurried out of the church with her head bowed. There was a rank of taxicabs standing at the edge of the little park. "Place Vendôme, if you please," she said. "Oui, Madame." The cab moved off. Carlotta closed her eyes hard against the lighted beauty of Paris, as if afraid that it would seduce her.

In her hotel room she sat by the open window and cried, not turning on the light. After some time she went to the chest of drawers and poured a drink from the Irish bottle. She returned to the window, glass in her hand. She was off schedule. More than an hour had passed since her last drink. Two hours, perhaps.

"*Slainte*," she said, looking at the glass in the half light that came through the window from the street.

Still, she did not drink the whiskey. She felt clear-headed, almost cold-blooded. "You are the creature," she said aloud. "You are the creature that lives in the bottle. It seems that you killed my father, who liked to drive a bright red car. But you killed him quick. Not the way you are killing poor Michael, slowly and with lots of pain. Not the way you are killing me, day by day, every day."

After nearly half an hour she went into the bathroom and poured the whiskey down the drain. She did the same with what was left in the bottle. She held the empty bottle in her hand, reading the familiar label.

"I don't think that you and I are going to be friends any longer," she said. "We are mortal enemies now, you and I."

She put the bottle on the bathroom floor and went back into the bedroom. The soft light from the window cast leafy shadows on the bedspread. I am sober, she said to herself. I am stone cold sober. She picked up the telephone and asked for Air France. "I want a seat to New York," she said.

"One moment, Madame."

When she had made the reservation she hung up the phone and stood beside the bed table. She was alone in the dark room and she was frightened. "I am sober," she said aloud. Stone cold sober. It is something I have done myself. But how long can I manage it this time? A month? Two months? Even a year? Still, there was Fowler and there were Fowler's pills. But I can't take one now. Somehow, for thirty-six hours, I must make it on my own, with no one to hold my hand.

She sat in the dark on the edge of her bed, afraid to move, waiting through the dawn and part of the day until it was time to call for a porter and get into a taxi for the drive to the airport. In the plane they were serving champagne. Carlotta sat beside a tiny window and stared at the sky.

In the taxicab at Idlewild she hesitated just for a moment.

"Okay lady, where will it be?" the driver said tolerantly.

"East Sixty-seventh Street in Manhattan," she said.

She gave him the number then sat back in the cab. It was nine o'clock on a Monday morning and the Parkway traffic was heavy but the stream of cars moved fast and very efficiently. Carlotta was calm, almost cold. She was following a thread of instinct started in the church of St. Germain des Prés, and it was no more than instinct now, but she was not frightened. She felt nothing until the moment a maid let her into her mother's house. Then the smells of childhood struck her and she had the blind urge to flee.

"Mrs. McBride," she said.

"And who is it that's calling, miss?" the maid asked doubtfully.

"I am her daughter," said Carlotta.

"You'll find her in the dining room then, miss," said the astonished servant.

"I know the way," Carlotta said.

She went downstairs and through the door into the low-ceilinged room. The glass doors to the garden were open and the smells of shrubbery and fresh earth came into the room. Alone at the head of the big table sat Mary Theresa Louisa McBride, dressed in black and wearing her pearls.

"Well, Carlotta," she said.

"Well, mother," said Carlotta.

For several seconds neither woman spoke. Then Carlotta said carefully, "If it is convenient, I should like to stay here in the house for a time."

"This is your home," her mother said.

The past hung in the air between them like a bomb and between them was a cloud of love and hate, more potent than any bomb.

"Thank you," said Carlotta.

"Would you like some breakfast?" asked her mother.

"Yes thank you, I am hungry," said Carlotta.

Her mother touched the bell and said, "Sit down and they will bring you something."

Carlotta took the chair she had used as a child. Her mother's face was calm above the pearls, but her fingers trembled as she broke a piece of toast, put butter on it, and spread it with marmalade.

How far back must I go? Carlotta asked herself, watching her mother's beautiful hands. Must I go all the way back to the day of my birth? Must I go back even further than that to the day of my conception? And how do I know that I will not take the wrong turning again, find myself running in blind flight? She was afraid. There was a risk.

But of course, she thought, there is always a risk. It is necessary to take risks and to make commitments that are primary, in fact to risk one's life, otherwise it is impossible to touch life or to live at all.

She thought of the whiskey she had poured away into the sewers of Paris, not much more than a day ago. How many more bottles would she pour down one drain or another before she declared herself the victor? She did not know. She thought of the prison room in Paris and of the scarred and naked body, limp and helpless on the dirty bed. She closed her eyes, then opened them. In her handbag were Fowler's pills, along with Katie's Irish passport and the letter from the detective agency. She opened the bag and took out the pills, shook one into her hand, looked at it, then swallowed it quickly. There was no taste, not even the taste of chalk. It is only a pill, she thought, a fat white pill with no taste. Still, it is something. It is an act that follows the other act of pouring the whiskey down the drain. She must, from now on, perform a series of such acts, for in this way she could demonstrate that she was living and not dead.

"Excuse me," she said, getting up from the table. "I must use the telephone."

She walked quite firmly into the pantry where there was a wall extension. She picked up the phone and dialed a number.

"Mr. Falkstein, please," she said.

"Who is calling?" the dispassionate voice inquired.

"Miss McBride," said Carlotta. "I am Carlotta McBride."

THE END